A DREAM OF HER OWN

Sarah Danbury is not very happy when her brother tells her he has arranged a marriage for her to the Earl of Weston, but she knows there is little she can do about it. At the Betrothal Ball, the Earl receives a message from one of his servants and, excusing himself, leaves Sarah standing alone. A stranger then approaches and, to her great surprise, tells Sarah that he has fallen in love with her and gently kisses her before departing. Sarah did not know it then, but she was to meet this mysterious man again in very different circumstances . . .

*Books by Barbara Best
in the Linford Romance Library:*

**THE HOUND OF TRURAN
WINGS OF DESTINY**

BARBARA BEST

A DREAM
OF HER OWN

Complete and Unabridged

LINFORD
Leicester

First Linford Edition
published 1997

British Library CIP Data

Best, Barbara
    A dream of her own.—Large print ed.—
Linford romance library
1. English fiction—20th century
2. Large type books
I. Title
823.9′14 [F]

ISBN 0–7089–7981–5

Published by
F. A. Thorpe (Publishing) Ltd.
Anstey, Leicestershire

Set by Words & Graphics Ltd.
Anstey, Leicestershire
Printed and bound in Great Britain by
T. J. Press (Padstow) Ltd., Padstow, Cornwall

This book is printed on acid-free paper

1

SARAH DANBURY stood before the study door, uncertain and a little afraid. What she was about to ask of her brother was going to be frowned upon, perhaps rejected outright. In this day and age a gently reared girl did not go against the norms of good behaviour, but this had to be done.

She straightened her shoulders and with grim determination, Sarah rapped on the door. She had come to the end of her tether and so desperate was she to leave this house, that her entrance was a little precipitant, displaying her frustrations, causing Bertram to look up startled, at this intrusion. She controlled herself, however, knowing she must do so, in front of this dearly loved brother.

"Bertie, I must talk to you," she said quickly, before her nerve failed her. "I — I don't want to hurt you, but I must get away from here," her voice dwindling, at the hurt, shocked expression on his face.

Bertram was of medium height, but over the years had become sadly rotund, which he refused to admit, except to say that he was a fine figure of a man, patting his watch chain, ignoring the extra links that had been added. When really amused, his hazel eyes would twinkle attractively, but lately, Sarah had noticed, this was not often. A frown was more likely.

He held a high position in Government, but was lax in the running of his home, quite content that Louise, his wife, should hold the reins in her capable hands. He was a pleasant, kindly man, a good provider, but had a stubborn streak, when it came to anything concerning his sister, having a deep loyalty for family matters. He was well aware that Sarah and Louise had never seen eye to eye, but failed to realize that his wife had made his sister, since coming under his roof, into nothing but a household drudge.

Shocked out of his early morning placidity, for he usually liked to sit here in his study and plan his day at the Ministry, he could only splutter. "You want to leave?" his sense of duty affronted. "But — but why and where would you go?"

Sarah held his gaze steadily. In any other situation she would have been amused at his ludicrous expression, his mouth open. "I'd like your permission and your blessing, to take up nursing as a career, at St. Thomas' Hospital." Suddenly her face radiated. "Oh, Bertie! Do you remember Mother reading from the newspaper cuttings that she had kept, about Miss Florence Nightingale going out to the Crimea and the wonderful work she and her nurses did for our wounded? Well, I'd like to become one of her nurses," her jaw jutting belligerently, to firmly add a clincher. "The nursing profession has now become respectable," daring him

3

to contradict her.

Still stunned, Bertram could only goggle, giving something like a snort. "Do you think you could manage Sarah, a gently reared girl like you? That life is a cruel grind, with very little thanks," raising an enquiring eyebrow.

"I'm very well suited to that here," came her quiet retort, her glance still meeting his steadily, losing none of its determination.

Bertram, fidgeting with his papers, had the grace to look a little sheepish, glancing quickly at the bracket clock on the wall.

He started up hastily. "My dear, I really haven't the time now, to discuss this with you, but I can assure you that I have not been remiss in thinking and planning for your future. I made a sacred oath to Mama, before she died, that I would be responsible for you. In a day or two," looking very pleased with himself, "I'll be able to be more specific," and with that, he picked up his case and rose ponderously to his feet. "I must leave now, or I'll be late for work and that will never do," and was gone, leaving Sarah gauping, her emerald eyes wide.

She sat down abruptly, sinking into an easy chair, thankful for this respite. "Well! What plans has Bertie made for me, I wonder?" When one lived in one's self, as much as she had had to do, one fell to talking out aloud. A bad habit, but it had the advantage of not having a bored listener, or any fear of contradiction. "Is Bertie thinking of sending me to my godmother in the depths of Wales?" and shuddered at the very thought, rising to her feet hurriedly.

Sarah managed to reach the drawing-room without having been missed and finished off the dusting. She had been a late baby, much cosseted by her parents and then her father had died, her mother not ever really recovering, until she too died, when Sarah was fourteen. The removal to Bertram's home had been traumatic enough, only

5

to find that Louise was an uncaring sister-in-law.

Louise, in her own way was a good wife and mother, but had been very much against the incursion of a young lady into the family circle and Sarah had become a thorn in her flesh, her Achilles' heel, because her young sister-in-law was so much more vivacious than Eunice her eldest daughter, although Priscilla, her youngest, showed promise of being a beauty. If Louise had had her way, other arrangements would have been made for Sarah, but for once, Bertram had been adamant.

Louise's other cross was the fact that she had been unable to produce a son and heir and this made her bitter and crotchety. No amount of comforting from Bertram had ever alleviated her sense of failure.

The young Sarah had been made to work, work that she had done willingly, deeply grateful that her brother had offered her a home, a kindly brother, but one who never saw what wasn't directly under his nose.

At eighteen, she still missed her mother sorely, but had been blessed with a delightful sense of the ridiculous, which had taken her over several hurdles in her short life, but the invidious situation in her brother's household left her, on occasions, exceedingly low. Her mother's loving heart had thought her only daughter beautiful, but she was a woman of sense and knew that to an outsider, Sarah was considered plain, so she had taken pains to nurture her sense of fun. The child of fourteen had, over the years, blossomed into a lovely woman.

Sarah's niece, Priscilla had been similarly blessed and here Sarah found a kindred spirit, although their times together, were naturally limited, as Priscilla was at school.

★ ★ ★

The whole family were at dinner, Sarah finding it impossible to conjure up any sort of appetite, as she took her place at the table, but only after quickly glancing around to see if everything was in order, the butler beginning to serve.

Several days had elapsed since Bertram's cryptic plans for her had been uttered and nothing further had been said. After dinner the family retired to the drawing-room, Sarah picking up Jane Austin's *Emma*, preferring it to Mansfield Park, settling herself into a comfy chair.

Bertram was standing before the fire. It had turned out to be a chilly evening and was warming his coat tails before its warmth, clearing his throat before saying quietly, but with pride. "Sarah, my dear, you'll be pleased to learn that I have been able to make a marriage arrangement for you," much gratified by everyone's response.

This news had come as a jolt to the whole family, Bertram, still smiling at their surprised faces. Evidently, not even Louise had been told of this latest development. It was Sarah who first found her tongue and had enough curiosity in her startled wits to enquire who the gentleman might be, in a tone that not even she recognised.

"Edward, Earl of Weston!" he replied triumphantly, with a pleased smirk.

"The Earl of Weston?" they all gasped.

Sarah protested in panic. "But — but I've only seen the Earl at functions, about three times in my life. He doesn't even know I exist!" She was babbling. "I've never had any conversation with him, so how does he even know what I'm like?" Suddenly all colour drained from her face. "Bertram, have I any say in this matter?" she asked anxiously, withdrawing with distaste at the very thought.

"I'm afraid not, my dear," aggrieved at her lack of appreciation. "It needs extremely delicate handling, to arrange such an alliance as this, especially with an eligible bachelor, one who would make you a good husband, my dear," he replied pompously, "and it would be a blow to the Earl's pride, if you now refused him, Sarah."

Bertram went across to where she was sitting, her book now on the floor, to pat her shoulder awkwardly, to enquire, "When you met the Earl, didn't you think him a very gentlemanly sort of man, my dear?"

"I didn't think of him at all," she replied slowly.

"Edward is an extremely nice man," smiling at her.

"How old is he?" asked Priscilla, a question nobody else had had the time to ask, still too bemused by this surprising announcement, to even open their mouths.

"About thirty-five, I should think, but — " began Bertram.

"That's old," she protested, rushing to place an arm around her aunt's shoulder. "Oh, Father, how could you!" she wailed.

"It's not you, he's to marry, Miss, so why the fuss?" cut in her mother blightingly.

Sarah swallowed hard, finding that her heart was beating high in her throat, her hands shaking. Trust Priscilla to get to the nub of the matter, but from a fifteen year old's perception, that was indeed old, ancient, in fact.

"What nonsense!" scoffed her father testily. "Edward is in his prime."

Eunice had also found her tongue, cutting in reproachfully. "Father, you could have kept the Earl for me," her mouth peevish, her voice plaintive. "After all, I'm only about six months younger than Sarah. Edward would have made me a charming husband, he's so handsome and rich. He'd give me everything I asked for and what is more, he would have allowed me to change my name to Euphemia," with a toss of her dark curls and a baleful look at her mother.

Priscilla giggled. "Then we would call you Phemie for short. Ugh!" pulling a face.

"You would not," Eunice cried out angrily. "You beast!"

"That is enough," rapped out her father. "Good Gad girl and don't dare throw a tantrum in my hearing." It was most unusual for him to speak so harshly to either of his daughters.

Eunice subsided into her chair with an envious mutter. "I would have liked to have been an old man's darling and to be fussed over, Papa."

"Hold your tongue, do! You're not yet eighteen," he replied, suddenly feeling threatened. It was Louise who usually dealt with family quarrels.

"My birthday is only a month away, Papa and why should Sarah have the chance of becoming a Countess?" her dark eyes stormy. "Nobody ever thinks of my needs."

Louise decided it was time to intervene and give her opinion, saying pacifyingly, "I agree with Eunice, dear. Edward would have been perfect for her."

Bertram rose to his feet, pulling down his waistcoat. "I've already made the arrangement with Edward and that's that," glaring at each member of his family in turn.

Another reason why he had chosen Edward for Sarah, was the prospect of his sister launching his two daughters into society, leaving him free of that burden. Sarah was a pretty little thing, with those strange green eyes and sensible into the bargain. She would make Edward a good wife. He sat down again and ordered tea, pleased that his sister had not made more of a fuss. He was proud of her.

Louise turned to her sister-in-law, her hazel eyes cold. "You can at least thank your brother for the trouble he has taken, Sarah. I hope you know that you are not really as beautiful as Eunice."

Priscilla, once more, flying to her aunt's defence. "She's lovely and has a sweet tongue," with a scowling glance at her sister. "And her kindness means a lot to me."

This made Sarah smile, as she turned to her brother. "Bertie, I'll try to be a dutiful sister and do appreciate what you have done on my behalf, but I don't love the Earl. Surely, one should have some softer feelings for the man you are about to marry?"

"Love!" snorted Louise. "My dear, love does not come into such arrangements. Edward is only marrying to produce an heir, pushed, no doubt, by the Countess. He has to do his duty and settle down. He would stare if you ever dared to discuss this with him."

Sarah turned again to Bertram, her eyes huge with concern. "Bertie?" her features lightening a little, at his sudden blush.

"Well, my dear," clearing his throat, "Of course there must be some finer feelings in these arrangements," with a softer look at his wife, "but perhaps not the love one reads about in romances," with a glance at the book, she was holding to her bosom.

"In Jane Austin's books, girls are not forced into marriage and are allowed to fall in love."

Bertram threw up his hands with a harried look at Louise. "Don't worry, dear. You and Edward will deal famously together," was all the comfort he could give her.

"Mama," broke in Priscilla, again throwing oil on troubled water. "Aunt will be able to take Eunice under her wing and chaperone her to all the parties that Sarah, herself will hold, once she is married and will do the same for me, when I am seventeen. Auntie, you will do that, won't you?" her eyes mischievous.

Sarah could only nod. Her youngest niece was a joy, with her endearing snub nose. A happy outgoing person, a fledgling trying out her wings.

Bertram held up his hand. "That's enough. This will be a very advantageous marriage for Sarah, whom I hope," with a slight smile, "will come to acknowledge this. I want to see you comfortably established."

"You've done well, dear," said Louise grudgingly. Sarah would no longer be a thorn in her flesh and that counted for a great deal. Often she had wished she could throw off this dislike she had for her young sister-in-law, but tensions drove her. At least she would be able to boast that her sister-in-law was Lady Weston.

Bertram became suddenly alarmed at Sarah's pallor. "But, my dear, you must have realised, that one day I would make arrangements for your future? I care about you," his eyes pleading for understanding.

Sarah pulled herself together and managed a smile. "I know, dear Bertie," she said submissively, rising to her feet. "Now, please excuse me. I am very tired."

As she left the room she heard Louise say, "Pity Eunice isn't the elder. I would dearly have liked Edward for a son-in-law," and gave an impatient sigh. "Oh, well!" Dismissing her daughters, she added curiously. "I suppose the money your mother left Sarah, will be adequate for her dowry?"

"I will not have to add to it. Be comforted, my dear," he said a little cynically.

Louise's mother had chosen Bertram Danbury for her only daughter realizing, with shrewd foresight, that he would not be offended by her occasional quirks and quiddities and that was the case, but in this matter, he was unusually irascible.

Louise, unheeding went on. "I still feel that Edward should have been for Eunice, our eldest daughter. An older man would best suit her and of course, Edward has a title."

"Eunice needs a few more years to curb that regrettable tongue of hers," he retorted tartly, "and if you could cure her of that Friday face, I'd be much obliged."

Louise wasn't listening. She had a burning desire that her husband would be rewarded for his dedicated devotion to his work in Government, in the form of a title. Sir Danbury! It sounded good and wondered, if perhaps, Edward would be of some help in this matter. Her spirits rose.

* * *

When Sarah went up to bed much later that evening, it was to find her youngest niece curled up on her bed. "Dear, you should be asleep by now," was her only comment.

Priscilla sat up suddenly. "What's happened? You — you look — " The words petered out. "You're not planning anything silly, are you? You're wearing your stubborn look."

Sarah smiled. "No, no, but I am determined that you will never have to accept an arranged marriage as I did tonight."

"Oh, could you?" with swift relief. "I — I have been worrying about that," she confessed, with a gulp. "But what could you do?"

"When you are of age, I shall only include young people in my invitations, to balls, morning dance parties, alfresco outings and I'll only invite the most eligible of young men," some of her worry lifting, to add with a smile. "And I'll give you permission to lose your heart to one of them." Priscilla was speechless, joy back in her blue eyes. "Now off you go to bed, or else we'll have Nurse looking for you."

Two evenings later, Sarah accompanied Bertram to the Earl's town house in St. James' Square and she was first introduced to the Countess and then to Edward, who took her limp hand in his, saying that he was most honoured, that she had consented to be his wife.

"My lord," was all she was able to murmur, barely raising her eyes to his face, but she did notice that he was taller than she was and that his smile was kind, before Bertram led her to where Lady Weston was sitting.

"My dear," she said, patting the place on the sofa next to her. "I'm extremely pleased to welcome you as my future daughter-in-law and have, over the months, noticed you particularly, at functions Edward and I have attended. We have both been impressed by your charming behaviour. Also, of course, you have unusual colouring, green eyes and tawny hair which my friends have commented on, also your vivaciousness, which I saw when you arrived, had been sadly quenched," her dark eyes sympathetic.

Sarah glowed at this praise. "Ah, that's more like," said the little Countess, with a friendly smile, before turning to enquire of Bertram how his family was.

This gave Sarah a chance to glance across at Edward, who came to sit next to her.

An even tempered man, was her assessment of him, but probably stubborn and caught his rueful grey eyes.

"Miss Sarah, this is not an easy occasion for you, or for me, either. I admit to a fellow feeling, for I have never asked a young lady to marry me before," with a twinkle in his lazy grey eyes, taking her hand in his firm clasp.

"Will you be my wife?"

She nodded, with a half smile. Should she say that she was honoured, or perhaps, that she was happy to accept his proposal, but the words stuck in her throat.

Lady Weston came to their rescue by offering Sarah a cup of tea, saying she was looking forward to getting to know her new daughter, in the days to follow.

That meeting was not of long duration, Bertram saying soon after tea, that they must be going, so as not to presume on any more of their time.

As they left, Edward asked if he might take her out driving the following afternoon. Sarah could only nod and smile her thanks, still with a strange sensation, that someone else was acting this part.

In the carriage on the way home, Bertram was jovially pleased with himself. "Well, I thought the meeting went off very well," he said with satisfaction, "but you had nothing to say for yourself, Sarah. Most unusual for you. Oh, I grant you this kind of meeting for a female, is awkward, but Edward is a likeable chap, don't you think?" his manner a little anxious.

"A — a female? I hate that word," on which she burst into a flood of tears, on his shoulder.

"Now, now, my dear," he admonished. "You've been taught, that in our class, this has to happen," patting her shoulder awkwardly.

"It's all so cold and unfeeling," shivering convulsively, as she sat up, to wipe her eyes.

"Edward won't rush his fences, he's not that stupid! You'll have your own home and, one day, children to comfort you. Sarah, I've always admired your determination to make the best of your situation, of which I have not been unmindful, dear. Please don't blame me. When Mother died it was the best solution for you."

She pulled herself together. He had

22

done his best and was grateful. "And if I don't produce a son?"

Fortunately they had arrived back home, Bertram thankful that he hadn't to answer that one.

★ ★ ★

As it turned out, the following afternoon proved to be most enjoyable for Sarah. The Earl was driving his curricle, a groom perched up behind him.

"Oh, what beautiful animals," she breathed, as he helped her into the carriage.

"Yes," he agreed, "and they are sweet goers, too," he said with pride. As they neared the park, Edward slowed down, drawing in his animals, turning to her. "Would you like to walk for a while? I'd like to get to know you better," and at her nod, asked his groom to take the reins, springing down to help Sarah dismount, offering his arm, holding her hand closely to him, as they strolled along in the warm sunshine.

"Sir, I'm afraid that I'm not really beautiful, or so I've been told and I'm sure you've had many opportunities of meeting some very lovely ladies."

His startled glance met hers, but there was no guile in those green depths. She had no idea that that remark of hers had been too close to the bone for his comfort.

"My name is Edward, Sarah," with a relieved smile, "I think you are a very beautiful young lady," and indeed, she looked charming in her lime green muslin, her straw hat lined with the same material, to make a pretty frame for her red-gold hair, in perfect harmony with the lovely afternoon, Edward more than happy to be in her company. He became a little anxious though, when she remained so silent. Most young ladies babbled too much.

"Are you perfectly happy with this arrangement?" he asked abruptly.

Sarah had a wild desire to burst out with, "You don't love me, you're only marrying to beget an heir," but his worried eyes stopped her. "I — I hope to become a conformable wife, Edward," she said primly, but with a softening of her expression.

He grinned suddenly, unexpectedly amused. "Thank you and I promise, as I shall do at the wedding ceremony, that I will be a good husband," to add with surprise, "For the first time in my life, I will be thinking of someone else's well-being, other than my own. A salutary lesson, I must say. Sarah, it was my choice that you be my bride. Bertram has a very high regard for your integrity and pleasing ways. These are the characteristics I want in my children," appreciating the colour sweep under her clear skin. "Besides, you have the most fascinating green eyes I've ever seen."

Those selfsame eyes twinkled so disconcertingly, at this fulsome praise, that he was a little taken aback, but made a quick recovery.

"I was not offering you Spanish

coin," he exclaimed, a little stiffly.

"Thank you," she replied, lowering her lashes demurely, which made him smile. Sarah Danbury certainly did not belong to the usual run of the mill young ladies and found that he was agreeably surprised in her.

As they continued their stroll through the park, heads were turned, ladies of the *haut ton* nodding their bonnets. They would soon see a notice of some importance in the daily newspapers.

Sarah found that Edward was a good conversationalist, enthralling her with stories of his overseas trips and was surprised how quickly the hour had flown, to find herself, once more, back home, where she introduced Edward to Louise and the two girls, admitting to herself, that she was feeling a little happier and willing to resign herself to the inevitable. The only remark she made after Edward had left, was that she liked Edward's kindly disposition.

"Well, that's what most women hope for," was Louise's only comment, but

Eunice once again began to rail against her father for not choosing Edward for her.

"Oh, bosh!" retorted her sister. "Your turn will come. Father, probably, has a gentleman in mind, even now. These matters take time, you know."

Sarah, smiling at this exchange, went up to change her gown, Priscilla joining her.

"Do you think you might be happy with Edward?" she demanded anxiously.

"Dear goose! I'll have to be, won't I?"

"I suppose so, but fortunately you're not one to be unhappy for long and candidly the Earl can't be worse than Mama and what you have had to put up with here," to continue excitedly. "You'll be Mistress of all Edward's properties and — and everything," ending up with a grin. "Did you notice how Mama and Eunice primped and preened in front of the Earl?" mimicking some of Eunice's die away expressions.

"Priscilla, dear, you shouldn't say such things!"

"Oh pooh! but what is Edward really like? I only saw him from an upstairs window when you left. Mama would have a fit!" with a giggle. "I at least noticed that his brown hair was not yet thinning on top and was well built. Too old for you, Auntie," she said disapprovingly.

Sarah smiled. "I found him interesting, with very nice manners and — "

"You mean he didn't try and kiss you on your first meeting?" her tone saucy.

Sarah chose to ignore this sally, but her mouth twitched. "He spoke most knowledgeably about some of his overseas trips and is an easy man to talk to. I was also agreeably surprised that Lady Weston is such a charming lady and one, I feel sure, I'll learn to love."

A comfortable silence fell, as Sarah changed and redid her hair, then turned to her niece. "Priscilla, I want to thank you now, for always being so supportive and for making my life here, bearable," giving her a hug.

"And I don't know what I will do without you, dear Auntie. You will invite me to visit you sometimes during the school holidays?" she asked anxiously. "I'll miss you," sudden tears in her voice.

Sarah nodded, tying a pinny around her neat waist. "Of course I will, when I need someone to laugh with me."

Priscilla suddenly looked scandalized. "You're not to do any more chores in this house!" with an authority that sat strangely on her young shoulders, her hands busy untying the apron strings. "Mary has already done your chores," with a pleased nod, her fair curls bobbing.

Sarah laughed, throwing the apron into the air, with gay abandon. "Come on, let's see what I have in my wardrobe that I may wear at my betrothal ball," she invited.

Priscilla's eyes widened. "You'll have

a new gown, of course," shock in her voice.

"I was thinking of the frock your Mama purchased for me, just the other day, for Melissa White's come out."

"Don't be silly! Papa will buy you a gown fit for a princess and isn't Eunice green with envy that Melissa is coming out before she is," rolling her eyes heavenward.

Sarah found that her life became far easier, Louise talking of nothing else, but the liberality that Eunice and Priscilla would enjoy after Sarah's marriage and was a far happier person, in consequence. So was Eunice, who could be sure of a glittering coming out party.

Sarah could only marvel at the fund of good nature that could be generated by the expectations of gifts, which she was expected to bestow, smiling wryly to herself.

★ ★ ★

The Countess, one morning, sent her own carriage for Sarah, with an invitation to visit her. As Sarah bowled along in comfort, she was quite overcome by this kindness. St. James' Square was reached, the carriage stopping in front of a beautiful house, that appeared, to Sarah, far more impressive, than the other evening when Bertram had brought her here, but perhaps she had been too nervous to appreciate it then. The butler opened the carriage door, with a bow and a smile, escorting her up the flight of steps, through the hall into a small drawing-room, where the Countess welcomed her with open arms, Sarah totally disarmed by Lady Weston's warmth. She was a petite little lady, with a wealth of dark curls, which she owed to her hairdresser and Sarah wondered how such a small person could have produced so large a son, her whole personality happy, making Sarah feel at ease, her eyes alert and kindly, accepting life as it came, with equanimity. A true English aristocrat to the tips of her tiny cream satin shoes.

A dear little pug, by the Countess' side, grinned up at Sarah. "Meet Peppy, my constant companion," she said, "and please sit down, my dear, here by my side on the sofa. He was a stray and well I know the tattle that goes on behind my back. Countesses should not own mongrels for pets, but he's a dear. The village lads had tied a brick to his neck and were about to throw him into the village pond."

Peppy nuzzled her hand, before making himself comfortable on his mistress' morning gown of lilac silk.

Lady Weston was a great talker and it was only after tea had been served, that Sarah had a chance to say with quiet determination, "My lady, I don't love your son." Had she been too abrupt, but relaxed when she saw that the Countess, instead of being offended at her lack of maidenly shyness, was viewing her with approval.

What a very unusual daughter-to-be Sarah was. There was no shyness there, that could have been expected in one so young. Her son could count himself fortunate in having found this charming girl, who, she was sure, if she read her character correctly, would not allow Edward to have all his own way.

"My dear, you're a daughter after my own heart," and gave a huge sigh. "What a relief, and thank you for sharing your concern with me, that is very natural," which brought a relieved smile from her guest, but Sarah was still concerned.

"My lady, the first time I have ever spoken to Edward was when Bertram brought me here to tea. Before that I had only seen him, at a distant at parties, that we both attended."

"And he noticed you, my dear," nodding. "Oh yes," seeing her surprise. "He told me about you and is very happy with the arrangement," beamed the Countess. "Welcome into the family, my dear," to add, "I too, know exactly what you are experiencing, for I did not love my husband, either,"

33

nodding. "Ours was also an arranged marriage and I'm afraid that I created quite a fuss," a girlish gurgle escaping her, "but Ivan and I learned, as the days turned into months, that love awakened and our marriage was a blessed one, because he was such a dear man. Edward takes after him, the same sleepy grey eyes, that view the world with a lazy tolerance, but for all that, my husband ran our properties well and Edward does the same. These characteristics will be passed on to his heirs. What's bred in the bone — but I have to admit there have been times when I could cheerfully have placed a fire cracker under him. Edward, the dear boy — "

Sarah found it hard to stifle a giggle, for her intended was at least, thirty-five years old.

"My dear, you'll have to be *firm*," snapping shut the tortoise-shell lorgnette that she used, to add force to her words, "but I have no wish to interfere in your lives and I shall retire to the

Dower House and await the arrival of my grandchildren," with a roguish gleam, to continue,

"I was very much addicted to romantic novels in my youth, but Sarah, I must warn you, that I found no passion that the poets speak of, but we found a quiet happiness and contentment. A loving glance across a crowded room, that made life worthwhile and of course watching Edward grow into a man. What I couldn't change, I endured, but looking back, I have no complaints.

"You must allow your personality to grow, Sarah and don't please, become a 'yes woman' for heaven's sake!" her glance sympathetic.

Sarah had relaxed. "Thank you, Lady Weston, for being so forthright and kind," smiling at this plump little lady. "I shall certainly do my best," she promised.

The Countess gave her a humorous glance. "I have a shrewd suspicion that you have a will of your own. Just feel your way for several weeks, which will be the most trying as you realise, with a shock, that you are mistress of this house."

Edward came in at that moment and Sarah rose to her feet, dropping a curtsy. "My lord," she murmured.

He hurried forward, raising her up, protesting with a smile. "Please don't ever do that again, Sarah. You are to be my wife and the name is Edward, remember?" seating himself beside her.

The Countess rang for more tea.

"Has Mother told you that I can be extremely pig-headed, but only when I feel very strongly about a matter?" with an affectionate glance in that lady's direction, who raised an eyebrow.

He had a nice smile, thought Sarah, her interest in her husband-to-be quickening much to her surprise and hoped that their future would be amicable, at least.

Edward had relaxed into a comfortable chair. "Sarah, do you wish to make a dash in town, or strive to the best lady whip?" he asked lazily.

"Not at the beginning," to blush rosily, adding hastily, "I'll have so much to learn and — Edward, you'll have to be patient with me."

"Of course, at least you'll be shot of that sister-in-law of yours. I would have disposed of her years ago, if I had been Bertram, but he seems happy enough."

Yes, she thought, because Louise sees that her tantrums do not reach Bertram's ears, careful that no ripple of the day should spill over when he was at home. At least her brother was contented.

"Edward, I think you do Louise an injustice. It is only me she dislikes. I've always been a thorn in her side and was against the idea of my going to live with them, but she's a good mother and keeps Bertram happy."

Edward's tea was brought in, giving his mother a chance to say, "Edward, you've been a good son and I shall expect you'll be that as a husband.

I've just been saying to Sarah, that as soon as you two are married, I shall retire gracefully to the Dower House. I already have plans for its redecoration and you Edward, will have no say in the matter. I'll become the Dowager Countess, so aging," with a chuckle, "and will look forward to my grandchildren," but to this, Edward would not agree.

"No Mother, please stay with us for a while. Sarah will need your help on how to go on and to introduce her to the families on our country estates."

Sarah agreed fervently. "Oh yes please, Lady Weston, I'd appreciate that," rising to take her leave. It sounded as if the Countess usually had her own way in most matters.

Edward helped her put on her silk spencer, that matched her dress, before she bade adieu to her hostess, dropping a shy kiss on her perfumed petal-like cheek, who gave her a hug and extracted a promise that Sarah would pay her another visit soon.

Edward was surprised at the stirring of his senses. Sarah was a dear little person and his approaching nuptials began to appear to be more attractive, softening his expression, mirroring his innermost thoughts.

Sarah was quick to notice this and was comforted. Their marriage would work and gave thanks for Lady Weston. She had heard too many stories about mothers-in-law ruling the roost, to such an extent, that their daughters-in-law became mere ciphers.

After Sarah and Edward had left, Lady Weston ordered another pot of tea, settled herself more comfortably in her chair, kicking off her shoes and as she did so dwelt on the satisfying supposition, that her son had given up that rapacious mistress of his. She had cost him a pretty penny, giving thanks that Sarah was no namby pamby Miss, hoping that Heaven would grant them an heir, or several, just to be on the safe side.

The tea tray arrived, her thoughts

wandering further. It had been most upsetting that Edward had been so dilatory in not marrying before, so as to produce a badly needed heir. What would have happened if her son had been killed? She relaxed and poured out a second cup of tea and started on a list of furniture which she would take to the Dower House, when the time came. Her eyes closed and she slept, a smile on her lips.

* * *

Edward accompanied Sarah home in the family carriage, Edward the first to speak, raising her hand to his lips. "I believe this marriage of ours, is going to be a success, so don't worry so, you anxious creature!" with a reassuring smile.

She was touched by his obvious sincerity, half smiled and nodded.

As they approached Mount Street, he drew her gently into his arms and kissed her. "You colour up most delightfully,

Miss Sarah Danbury, just like a pink carnation," his voice pleasantly amused. "Your first kiss, Sarah?"

She nodded, unable to meet his teasing eyes, but was rewarded by her reluctant grin.

"Ah, that's much better," he approved. "We'll deal very well in harness, my dear."

The carriage stopped, Edward only accompanying her to the door, saying he had an appointment with his bailiff, waiting until she was met by the butler.

Lenten gave her a fatherly look of approval, before she slipped past him to go upstairs, thankful that Priscilla had not seen her arrival. Her niece was the last person she needed.

Sitting on the window seat, with her hot cheeks against the cool pane, she relived that kiss, so very different from the kisses Bertram had given her on her birthday and at Christmas, grateful that Edward did not have a moustache and gave a nervous giggle. She had regained her poise by the time Priscilla entered and was able to tell her about her visit to the Countess and that Edward had seen her home, of the opinion that they would run in harness, famously.

"For all the world as if you were a horse," Priscilla said indignantly. "I have heard the Earl is a bruising rider to hounds and that, probably, colours his language. You'll have to get used to it, Auntie," was that damsel's sage comment, to add eagerly, "Well, has he kissed you yet," she demanded.

Sarah nodded. "And what do you know about kisses, Miss, might I ask?"

Priscilla tossed her hair over one shoulder, to say with smug satisfaction. "I've been kissed before," settling herself beside Sarah. "He said I had the most enchanting curl to my lips when I was amused," with a giggle.

Sarah stared at her. "But — but, when, who — ?" viewing, with misgivings, her niece's mischievous face. In a few years, this niece of hers was going to be a beautiful young lady and quailed at the thought, that she would be Priscilla's chaperone at all the functions that she would be giving for her nieces, when she was expected to launch them into society.

"The drawing master," Priscilla said with a twinkle, "I rather liked it. Did you enjoy Edward's?" inquisitively.

"I — I don't know. It was so sudden and landed on my cheek."

"You must have moved," knowledgeably. "You'll get used to it," was her niece's incorrigible comment.

The date of the betrothal ball was announced soon after Sarah's visit to the Countess and all the invitations were sent out by Lady Weston's secretary, Louise and Eunice indulging in grandiose schemes, for Eunice's coming out party in which Sarah was to figure prominently.

Sarah's ball gown in pale peach mousseline was duly delivered. The tiny puffed sleeves and wide scalloped neckline, suited her slim figure to perfection. The outer dress was knee length, to show off the flounces of the satin petticoat in a darker shade, which suited her tawny hair and green eyes.

Louise had wanted her dressed in white, as befitting every young lady, but both her husband and her daughters had overruled her.

"Can't have the gel dressed in white, with that mop of red hair!" Bertram had differed, "and anyway, she's already out."

"It's not red, Papa," protested Priscilla, loyally. "It's more gold than red and her lovely creamy skin is not that of a redhead, either."

Louise had shrugged and given in gracefully, allowing that the colour was most attractive and suited Sarah.

The day of the ball arrived, Priscilla told not to wake Sarah too early, much to Priscilla's surprise. Her mother was not usually so kind but, in any case, Sarah was awake.

The day she had dreaded was upon her. An engaged girl should be happy, but all she could feel was a debilitating lack of energy and the day had not yet begun. Pulling herself together, she dressed and made her way to the breakfast table, where Eunice found her, scandalized at the good breakfast she was making. "Soused herrings, baked eggs and toast, spread with orange conserve, how could you, Sarah!" she said in a failing voice, slumping into a chair.

"I'm feeling much better already," she replied airily.

"But what about tonight? Aren't you dreadfully nervous?" spreading butter on a slice of bread.

"Tonight is a long way away and I've decided that I'll not worry about today or the tomorrows," ending up with a determined grin.

Louise had decided that she would dress Sarah herself, in Louise' own bedroom, with its numerous mirrors and dainty furnishings, Priscilla curled up on the day bed, determined to miss nothing, exchanging roguish glances with her aunt, while enviously admiring Sarah's beautiful gown.

Sarah had chosen to wear her hair piled on top of her shapely head, held in place by a circlet of frilled net and silk flowers, in colours to match her gown, her fringe cut just above her mobile eyebrows, which lent her face a puckish look.

"Oh, Sarah!" breathed Priscilla, "you're beautiful," glancing down at, what she called, her too girlish sprigged muslin, pulling a disgusted face, but at least, she had been invited to the ball and at her age, too.

Sarah stood in front of the large, gilt framed mirror, with no feelings at all. This tall, slim girl, with tawny hair and green eyes, soon to become betrothed to the Earl of Weston this very night, was not the real Sarah and she shuddered convulsively.

She did react, though, with unusual irritation, when Louise started fussing about the hem being not quite even. She didn't care at all, so why should anyone else?

Priscilla quick to notice this, piped

up, "Cheer up, Auntie, you look as if you are about to attend a funeral."

This did call forth a slight smile, but there was no good pretending to be delighted at the thought of this evening. It was only Louise and her plans for Eunice, who were going to benefit.

Sarah had never been able to stand for any length of time, her mother usually having to bolster her up, with egg nogs and brandy, whenever the dressmaker had paid them a visit.

Suddenly, Sarah could stand no more and hurriedly sat down, not caring if her dress did get crushed. Even Louise looked a little worried at seeing her pallor and asked Priscilla to order tea and biscuits.

"And we all might as well, have some."

It was Priscilla who waved a vinaigrette under her aunt's nose, worried that Sarah was so close to tears, curling her hand into her limp one. "You'll feel more the thing when you've had your tea," she murmured. "Ah, here it is now," looking around. "Annie, thank you. Please pour some for Miss Sarah quickly. There's a dear."

"Oh, Miss Sarah!" sighed the little maid, eyes as round as saucers. "You do look a treat!"

Mrs. Smeeth, the housekeeper, bustled in, congratulating Sarah, saying she would be the belle of the ball and make no mistake about that.

"Me and Lenten and all the staff, wish you everything of the best, my dearie," wiping her eyes on the corner of her apron, to say later to Lenten, "I have me doubts as to whether Miss Sarah is happy," ending with a sniff.

After Sarah had dressed, Bertram came through, bringing with him a leather case which he opened on the dressing table. There lay, in all its beauty, a string of well-matched pearls, with a diamond clasp.

"Mama's pearls!" she cried, with delight. "Are these for me?" gently tracing the pearls, with a rosy tipped finger and when he nodded, "Please put them on for me. Oh, how the memories come back! These were Father's gift to Mama on her twenty-first birthday. Now they are mine and I'll cherish them all my life," again trying to hold back tears. "Thank you for keeping them for me, Bertie." She remembered them so well on her mother, who always came into her bedroom before she and her father attended to balls, when she was small.

Louise's only comment was, "A very fine string."

And Priscilla's? "I wouldn't mind owning pearls like that, myself. Oh, look, Eunice how they glow against Sarah's skin," turning around. "Where's she gone?"

Eunice was sulking in her room, angry that it wasn't herself in that lovely ball gown, about to be betrothed to the Earl of Weston. No doubt when her turn came, she would be fobbed off, with a commoner.

"They are at least your own, dear

Sarah and not an heirloom belonging to the Weston family," commented Bertie acidly.

His pride had been sorely battered, by the fact that Sarah's ball was being given by the Countess and not by himself. Lady Weston took too much on herself, in his opinion. Louise had not supported him in this and her accurate remark that the Earl's home in St. James' Square, was far more suitable than their own home in Mount Street. Even his daughters had not supported him in this, which had sent him striding furiously to the sanctuary of his study.

He had been slightly mollified when Sarah had followed him, agreeing that she would have been far more comfortable in their smaller ballroom.

"Now Louise will want something bigger when the girls come out," he had growled.

"Not Priscilla, Bertie," stoutly defending her youngest niece. "And remember, I will be expected to launch the girls from my own home," which did not exactly mend matters. She had added quietly, "I'll be very willing to entertain on a large scale. That will enable the girls to meet eligible young men and leave you free from worry."

"Please leave Priscilla with us a little while longer. That ray of sunshine leavens the lump," he had pleaded, "but we'll have to watch that quirky sense of humour," he had warned.

"I'll do nothing of the kind, Bertie," she had retorted. "In this too starchy age, she's a breath of fresh air. Life is one laugh with her."

"Joke, you mean," he had muttered, "and there is the task of providing Eunice with a marriage partner. Not a simple task, with her saucy tongue and die away airs."

"Well, she does want to be an old man's darling," she had gurgled.

"You're a good sort, Sarah and I hope, sincerely, you will be happy with Edward."

Bertram had another problem. Only

this morning, a note had been handed to him, stating that the Countess would be sending around her own coach to convey the family to the ball.

Bertram had exploded. Did her ladyship think that his carriage was not good enough to be seen in front of her front door? and had ground his teeth in frustration.

Louise once again, had not agreed. "Sarah's dress will not get so crushed in a larger carriage."

She had been very grateful to Lady Weston for holding the ball at her town house, shuddering to think of all the organising that would have fallen on her shoulders. Their ballroom would have proved to be quite inadequate. She turned from Sarah, satisfied at the picture she presented, her glance going to her eldest daughter.

"Eunice!" she said despairingly. "You haven't persevered with that Citron Water I told you to use for those freckles. In this light they are most pronounced."

"I think that flight of freckles across your retroussé nose is most attractive," Sarah said kindly, but her niece was not satisfied, sticking out her full bottom lip.

"I did ask you, Mama, to take me to that doctor on the Continent, who deals with skin problems, but you wouldn't listen," she replied sullenly.

"Come on, ladies. It's time to leave," called out Bertram impatiently. "We dare not be late."

Eventually, everyone was bestowed in the spacious coach and were driven away, to slow down a little later Bertram leaning forward to point out the Weston's mansion.

Priscilla gasped. "You'll be living here, Sarah?" awe in her words, her thickly lashed blue eyes sparkling from the blaze of lights in the street, as the carriage drew to a halt, lackeys springing forward to hold the horses.

2

OF all the lovely mansions in this square, the Earl of Weston's must surely be the most impressive, thought Louise, as the family were helped out of the luxuriously upholstered coach, by a footman who must have been watching out for them, Priscilla awed by the amount of carriages disgorging guests, link boys holding lighted torches, dashing about trying to ease the flow of traffic, flambeau's spewing light from their holders on the walls of the house, rivalling all the lamps in the street and the general air of expectancy as they walked up the royal blue carpeted steps, to the massive double oak doors, which had been flung open wide for the occasion.

They were met by the old butler, introducing himself as Norton, bowing to Sarah saying how very happy they all were, that Master Edward was at last, going to bring home a lovely bride.

He led the way out of the small reception area into the hall, the chandeliers lighting up the room, as bright as day.

It was a vast room, for what it was, with marble tiles in beige and light green, masses of flowers banking one wall and a beautiful carved staircase, ascending to the upper floor. If this was the hall, what must the other reception rooms be like, wondered Louise, regret again filling her, that it wasn't Eunice who would be mistress of this lovely home.

A footman, very smart in red and gold livery, approached, presenting Sarah and the other ladies, with posies of hot-house flowers, nestling in beds of maiden hair fern.

As Bertram and Sarah had already visited the house, the room did not have such an effect on them, as it had for the others. The ladies had been silenced, until Priscilla murmured to Sarah, "Pomp and ceremony!" holding on tightly to her hand. It was the first function she had ever attended and was a little nervous. "Look at this lovely tiled floor. Anyone for hopscotch?" she asked irrepressibly, in a loud whisper and was promptly told to 'shush' by her mother, but the butler had heard and smiled as he handed the ladies over to a small, plump, pleasant faced woman, who led them upstairs.

Priscilla hung back, for a moment, to admire the line of family portraits, that appeared to march with them up to the wide gallery, on the second floor, stifling a giggle. Evidently, it was the rule of the house, that their portraits had only been commissioned when they were old. Most of the men must have been, what her father called, pompous asses and as for their wives, well! They all looked so stern and forbidding. Sarah would certainly not look like that. She would smile, refusing to conform to any dictates, by the painter.

She murmured, naughtily, to Sarah. "You'll know what Edward will look like in the years to come."

They were shown into a well appointed Powder Room, where they were able to leave their shawls. Louise glanced quickly at the three young ladies, but their dresses had not been crushed and was pleased that they were all sporting reticules of fine gold mesh, presented to them by her husband.

"Why should Sarah have pearls and a reticule?" Eunice asked waspishly, but nobody had paid the least attention to her.

As the ladies made their way downstairs again, the butler stepped forward and asked them, including Bertram, who had been talking to an old friend, to follow him, escorting them to Lady Weston's private drawing-room, where the Countess and Edward were waiting, welcoming the family.

"Now, my dears," said Lady Weston, "It is time for you all to meet our guests," turning to the butler to give him certain orders to that effect.

"Oh, lor'!" thought Sarah, inelegantly, stifling a nervous reaction, not daring to look at her niece.

The two families lined up and the welcoming ceremony began, Priscilla thrilled when a young gentleman, Kim Philpot, shook her hand and said in a low voice. "I'll take up your offer of hopscotch, Miss Priscilla Danbury, if you'll allow me a few dances?"

She had only time to grin and nod, her eyes sparkling, as she watched him walk away, before the next couple shook her hand.

At last all the guests were in the ball-room, their hostess seating Bertram and his family.

"Thank goodness, that's over," murmured Edward, beckoning the butler who was making his stately way in their direction, carrying a tray of champagne, but Sarah and her family, for the time being, were more interested in admiring the beautiful room, tastefully decorated in ivory and gold, with matching drapes at all the tall glass doors, flung back, to reveal a wide verandah, that led into a garden, festooned with lanterns. Once again masses of flowers, all in pastel shades, were arranged against the silk lined walls.

"How magnificent!" murmured Louise to her husband, who had a hollowness in his middle, at the thought that he would be asked to have their ball-room redecorated.

At a signal from Lady Weston, the band of the Royal Marines struck up the first waltz.

Edward rose to his feet to claim Sarah. "This is your very own ball, my dear," bowing and offering her his arm, to take her on to the dance floor. "And may I say that I'm very proud to be leading out such a beautiful young lady?" kissing her hand, punctiliously. "Come, let's open your ball," swinging her into the waltz, Sarah gratified at the depth of sincerity in his deep voice.

Edward danced beautifully, Sarah

commenting on this, exhilaration filling her as they dipped and swayed, through the throng of guests, all enjoying Herr Strauss' lovely waltz.

"I had ample opportunity as a young man — "

"And you in your dotage, Sir?"

He grinned down at her sally. "I can give you seventeen years, Sarah. Does that seem old to you?" his tone a little anxious.

She shook her head. "You are making me feel like thistledown."

His arm tightened, her body unnervingly close to his.

"You feel far more than that," he murmured with satisfaction. "Can't stand pole-thin females, which seems to be the fashion now, more's the pity. A man needs something more substantial." He paused, to guide her through a knot of dancers. "It is strange," he mused, "that I have never conversed with you, at all the functions we both have attended, but that is not to say, that I never noticed you, Sarah," he hastened to add.

"Perhaps I was too young for you, Edward?" keeping her words playful and a smile pinned to her lips. "You must have preferred more sophisticated ladies?" For all her effort, she could not stop cynicism creeping through.

He nodded ruefully. "But since I've met you, Sarah, I've found you delightfully fresh and I'm more than happy to have you for my wife and the mother of my children."

Sarah lowered her eyes. Edward was only marrying her to beget an heir. It was his duty, not noticing several envious glances watching their progress.

Edward murmured, close to her ear. "I've been thinking of your position, my dear, which can't be an easy one and would like to suggest that I court you, after our marriage, which, by the way, my mother has arranged for next month."

She raised surprised eyes to his. "Would you do that for me?" touched by this thoughtfulness.

His smile was warm. "I think you're worrying that you don't love me; don't even know me! I'll teach you all that," he promised.

She turned her head quickly into his shoulder, the couples around them smiling and nodding, as his arm tightened around her slim body.

The dance ended and he took Sarah back to where his mother was sitting, saying he would bring her a drink.

Lady Weston patted her hand, kindly. "My dear, you look lovely. I'm very satisfied with my daughter-in-law to be."

Sarah thanked her, to say quietly, "I'll do my best to make your son happy, Ma'am," with a smile.

"You must get Edward to show you around our estate and the succession houses of which we are both very proud, but that will have to be for another day, won't it?" she confided archly.

Sarah was beginning to feel more at home and began to enjoy the ball, a young gentleman claiming her, saying teasingly, that she wasn't yet married. She hastily looked around for Edward, caught his eye and nod and gave her card to several young gentlemen, who had come to ask for a dance.

The chaperones and other elderly ladies, who made up a large part of the guests, rejoiced that Mary had been able to procure such a beautiful girl for her only son, for they all liked the Countess, except Gussy Springfield, who never had a kind word to say about anyone, anyway.

Meanwhile, Priscilla was highly gratified when Kim Philpot came to claim his dance, to write his name against several numbers.

"I really shouldn't be dancing," she confessed, "But Mother thought that, because I'm family, it would be permissable," beaming up at him. "Is that hair of yours, that much unmanageable, or is it the fashion? I'm not out yet, so I'm not in the know," brimming over with vivacity.

Mr. Philpot chose to be amused. "Now that's enough sauce from you, young Priscilla, but this I will say, you dance very well. By the way, how old are you, if I might ask? You're certainly not shy, which is a change, believe you me," he said with exaggerated feeling.

"Fifteen and a bit," came the prompt reply, "And you're only a few years older. May I call you Kim, or is that frowned upon, too?"

"Of course you may use my given name and I'm still willing to take up your invitation to play hopscotch in the hall?"

Priscilla chuckled. "I wondered if you meant what you said," and at his nod, "Let's go then," coming to a halt, as he grabbed her arm.

"No, I want to finish this dance with you." It was a mad romp, that both enjoyed immensely and at its end, he said, "Now, come let's go," catching her hand in his. "Wonder what old Norton will say. He's a stickler!"

Norton, coming into the hall, some

time later, paused startled, his mouth turning up at the corners, as he hurried out again to give certain orders, one being wooden counters to be made by the estate carpenter and then rounded up several other young people, Eunice amongst them, inviting them to partake in a parlour game.

Meanwhile Edward was taking Sarah to the conservatory to cool down after a hectic dance, but as she stopped at one of the open doors to drink in the cool breeze, a waiter came over to whisper in Edward's ear, who began to look very perturbed and agitated.

He turned to her apologetically. "My dear, a matter has cropped up which needs my immediate attention. Please excuse me. Would you mind waiting in the conservatory for me?" patting her arm, but his thoughts were obviously elsewhere.

Sarah nodded, Edward walking off, but she continued to stand by the door, watching the colourful scene before her. Most of the ladies' dresses were superb and must have cost their owners a great deal of money.

A late-comer arrived, a footman ushering him into the ballroom, reminding him gently, that he was a little late, a remark that was ignored, the gentleman casually looking around him, his glance eventually, finding Sarah. He stiffened, watching her intently, as if he had suffered some shock.

"May I know who that lady is, standing by that open door, watching the dancing?" he demanded suddenly.

"You must be a newcomer to these parts, Sir," surprised. "She is Lord Weston's fianced bride," admiring his tall elegant figure, in his black evening attire, his white cravat exquisitely tied, his dark hair just so.

A friendly little spinster, who was sitting close by and having heard the gentleman's question, leaned over. "Isn't she beautiful? Edward is most fortunate! Go and congratulate her," shooing him away with a flutter of her tiny hands. "She's the dearest girl and so friendly."

The footman had left to attend to another late-comer the gentleman walking to where Sarah was standing.

Sarah, watching the dancing, had began to wonder if this was all a dream. It was as if her other self was looking down on this throng of people; at the young, tawny headed girl, with green eyes and who was gowned so beautifully. Nothing was real! She quickly shook off this fanciful mood, coming back to reality as she watched yet another guest approach her, liking what she saw and as he came nearer, noticed that he had very deep blue eyes and waited for his congratulations, but none came.

He took her hands in his warm clasp, his gaze widening in wonderment.

She frowned a query. The gentleman had not yet spoken a word and she was beginning to feel a little uncomfortable at his intense scrutiny, his eyes so tender, though intent, Sarah having a strange feeling that he was trying to imprint her features on his memory. She should really terminate this meeting, but could find no words. Where was Edward? This guest must surely be a family member.

When he did speak, his words puzzled her.

"It's just my confounded luck that I've found you too late," his tone so sincere that she could take no offense. "What I'm about to say may surprise you, I'm surprised myself, but there is an inner force that I cannot gainsay. Bear with me. Across a crowded ballroom I knew, in a moment of time, that I had seen the one woman, whom I would love for a life time and it's too late," smiling a little bleakly, at her startled face. "You'll always be in my heart. I just want you to know that," he said simply.

"I'm sorry," were the only inadequate words she could utter, extremely aware of his sensitive, revealing face. He really meant what he was saying!

He nodded. "I too, am sorry. You don't know what this means to me. The old sage says, 'that it is better to have loved and lost, than never having loved at all', but how am I going to live without you?" he groaned.

Sarah felt the colour run under her fair skin, strangely loathe to break this spell that had her in its grip, wondering at the strange breathlessness that had caught her unawares.

The stranger went on, "I wish you all the best in the world," gently drawing her into his arms, bending his head to kiss her lingeringly on her surprised mouth, the sweetest kiss, holding her to him as if she were the most fragile creature in all the world, looking deep into her eyes, his glance roaming her flowerlike countenance.

"Forgive me, but every word is true. I can no more stop myself from blurting out these words, than I can stop the tides of the sea. I won't see you again, but I'll always love you," releasing her reluctantly, to give her another searching look before striding away, to disappear into the crowd, without a backward glance.

Sarah finally came back to earth, her lips still tingling from that gentle kiss, to glance around her quickly. Nobody was taking the least notice of her and wondered again, what had happened to Edward. He had no right to leave her for so long. Turning, she entered the conservatory to sink back limply on to a seat, becoming a little worried, but comforted herself with the fact that the stranger's height and well-built body, must have shielded her from any curious gaze. If someone had seen them, they would have probably, thought he was a friend of her family, congratulating her on her betrothal. Her fingers went up to her lips. She hadn't had much experience of being kissed, but knew that she would never forget this experience. Would Edward ever kiss her like that, she wondered. It had been very real and very sweet, her senses strangely aroused.

A nervous giggle escaped her. Edward was rather cold, she guessed, or perhaps he too, wasn't best pleased at his mother's insistence, that he do his duty to his name. A hot wave of colour swept her cheeks. Why hadn't she drawn back from the stranger's embrace, her maidenly modesty offended, but she had been incapable of any such action, mesmerized by the tenderness in his eyes and then that kiss? Would she ever respond to Edward's as she had done to the stranger's and a smidgen of regret assailed her.

She sat up suddenly as two people entered the conservatory, both surprised and a little concerned to find her alone.

"My dear, where's Edward?" the lady looking around her. "Why are you here by yourself?" she asked, sitting down beside Sarah, with a flurry of petticoats, to add quickly, "I'm Anne Brownlee and this is my husband, Bruce. We came to get away from that dreadful crush and the heat," fanning herself vigorously.

"I think I heard something about a horse," supplied her husband, "And you know what Edward is like."

Sarah, pleased to have her mind taken off her past experience, replied that Edward had excused himself, as some urgent business had come up.

Mr. Brownlee nodded, sagely. "That's Edward! I do hope, Miss Danbury, that you will teach him that he really has to think of others," he remarked dryly.

"He is rather selfish, I'm afraid," agreed Mrs. Brownlee sympathetically, patting Sarah's knee.

At that moment Edward arrived, very apologetic and not a little sheepish. He greeted the Brownlees, who made a quick retreat, the lady murmuring quietly, but firmly to Sarah, "Begin *now*, dear," pressing a kindly hand on her shoulder.

As they left, Edward eyed Sarah a little uncertainly. "Please forgive me for neglecting you so shamefully. Glad that

Anne and Bruce kept you company. Nice couple."

Sarah took pity on him, noticing that he appeared to be a lot more cheerful and asked if he had sorted out his problems.

"Yes, indeed!" he said eagerly, seating himself beside her. "It was my favourite hunter, you know, but she's much better now, thank goodness! We have a lovely little mare," quite unaware of her rising indignation.

"You — you left me for a foaling?" she gasped. "Oh!" biting her lip to stop herself from exploding.

"My dear," sighing ruefully, noticing her indignation, "You'll have to take me in hand. This is all new to me," his expression so contrite, that she suddenly felt a bubble of laughter burst.

However, Edward was annoyed. "It's no laughing matter, Sarah. That foaling was very important to me," he retorted snappishly, his lips firming.

"Even to leave me here for so long,

Edward?" her eyes unwavering, to end with a resigned sigh. "It is just as well that I have this ridiculous sense of humour, for I'm beginning to think that it might be our saving grace. Come, Edward," she coaxed, tucking a friendly hand under his arm. "Let's join in the dancing again. I'm perfectly rested and cool," with a pointed look at his hot face.

Edward had calmed down, thankful that Sarah had been so accommodating and hadn't enacted a scene, which she could have done, patting her hand and again apologizing, saying he hadn't yet realised fully that he now had her to consider. "Come, my dear, I'll take you to Mother. It is time to announce our betrothal," giving her a charming smile.

There was a roll of drums and an expectant hush fell, as Edward led Sarah on to the dais, placing the family cluster ring on her finger, that had a moment before, graced the hand of the Countess.

Edward raised his voice. "Ladies and gentlemen, I have great pleasure in announcing our engagement and I know we both have all your good wishes for a very happy marriage. I must also say, that my bride-to-be is a very charming young lady, one which we are very pleased to welcome into our family and thank you for your presence here, making this evening such a memorable one."

Most of the guests gathered around the young couple, several ribald remarks made, but the general consensus of opinion amongst the males, was that Edward was a lucky dog and didn't really deserve such a honey of a girl; Lady Weston, Bertram and family, being the first to congratulate the happy pair.

The band struck up, Edward sweeping Sarah into the dance, the guests following. It was just another function in the present London Season.

Edward danced with Sarah several times during the course of the evening, her dance card gratifyingly full, but even so Sarah felt a little out of place amongst all the lovely ladies, feeling sure that she was the object of conjecture. It never occurred to her, that quite a few of those ladies, were fiercely jealous of her freshness and for winning the most eligible man in London.

"So, Weston has at last taken the plunge, poor devil," this from a gentleman, sporting side whiskers which he stroked from time to time. "Charles, are you coming with me to Lady Cartwright's drum, or are you staying here? Damned dull! Or we could visit that place in Soho, which might be more to your liking," and the two men discreetly, left.

Sarah was beginning to feel the heat generated by the hundreds of candles in the giant chandeliers which lit this huge room, a tiredness that ran through her slim body and longed for the ball to end. Her partner was not helping matters, either. He was an old roué she thought, his conversation not suited to her taste.

"Edward is such an old stick, my dear and you're a delightful filly — " He paused seeing the shocked disgust in her widening eyes, ignoring her outraged gasp. "You'll come around to my way of thinking," he said cynically.

Could she just walk off and refuse to dance with this man, she wondered, looking around for Louise, but could not see her. Fortunately the Countess had seen her distress and looked around for her son. What on earth had that man said to that sweet child? Edward should be looking after Sarah and not allowing that rapscallion, Lord Rigley to dance with her. He was known for his bad manners and innuendos, she fumed and rose from her chair, to beckon her butler.

Several terse orders made him tread carefully through the dancers, to murmur a few words into his lordship's ear, who goodhumouredly, led Sarah to where Lady Weston was standing.

"Ah, Rigley! I'm desolate to terminate your dance, but I have to introduce Sarah to a very old friend of mine. I'm sure you'll not mind?" she enquired sweetly, her eyes challenging him to utter one word in protest.

He bowed, amusement on his lined, raddled face. "I quite understand your concern, Countess and bow to your superior judgement," and with that was gone.

Lady Weston sighed. "I knew Rigley when I was much younger. A charming man then, but has gone off sadly. My dear, I am sorry you had to bear with him."

"Thank you for rescuing me, Lady Weston. I — I didn't quite know what to do and my sister-in-law wasn't in sight," finding that her hands were trembling.

"Come with me child, and we'll go and have a cup of tea," guiding Sarah by the arm to the refreshment area.

Louise had been sitting with a friend and so engrossed was she by what was being said, that she had forgotten her chaperone duties. She quickly glanced around the ballroom. Sarah was sitting quietly by the Countess, but where were her two daughters?

The last she had seen of Priscilla, she was dancing with a gangling youth, with shockingly untidy hair and Eunice had been sitting next to her, but she too seemed to have vanished. Were they in the garden?

The butler seeing her concern, whispered something in her ear. With an unbelieving stare, she followed him into the hall, the noise there was deafening, as the butler opened the door. The hall was filled with happy young people, Eunice and Priscilla amongst them, a lot of them playing hopscotch, with wooden counters, the housekeeper presiding over the activities, two grinning maids standing by a large white clothed trestle table, laden with delicious bits and pieces that young people enjoyed.

Louise quietly shutting the door,

remembered her youngest daughter's remark and smiled. They would come to no harm there and perhaps some good contacts would be made, she thought, ever optimistic.

★ ★ ★

Later in the evening, Edward took Sarah into his study, seating her in a comfortable chair. She was very impressed and pleased at the amount of books the shelves held. At least she would be able to indulge her love of reading and perhaps here, she and Edward could find common ground.

He had gone to a small wall safe. "I have a gift for you, my dear," laying a jewellery box on the desk. "It comes with my love," his voice matter of fact, as he placed the necklace around her neck, his breath on her nape, to turn her around to face the mirror, saying, "This is a family heirloom."

"Just in case I should decide to pawn it?"

He chuckled. "I hope not, but I like your sense of fun."

Sarah stared at her reflection, raising her fingers to touch the beautiful stones. "Edward, I'm honoured! It's beautiful."

The necklace was designed in a daisy pattern, each small flower outlined and joined together by gold filigree, the petals tiny diamonds, the centres rubies.

He smiled. "My dear, your eyes rival the sparkle of those gems." He paused to continue a trifle diffidently. "Sarah, you don't regret our engagement, do you?" he asked again, pleased when she shook her head and smiled.

"No, Edward, I don't, for I've come to accept what was meant for me, but I must be honest with you. I was appalled when Bertie told me that he had made arrangements for our marriage and thought of the countless women who are left on country estates, to breed and bring up their families, while their spouses philander in town.

Edward," with a very level look from her fine eyes, "I'll not tolerate that kind of treatment."

For a moment he was so taken aback by this plain speaking, that he remained silent, but respect for this young girl, was born. He chuckled. "You're going to be just like my Mama. She never tolerated that behaviour, either. Not," he made haste to add, "that Father would ever dare put a foot wrong in that direction. Come, let's join the dancers again, we've become far too serious."

The ball drew to a close, Norton asking the young people to go back to the ballroom, as the hall would soon be filled with departing guests.

Kim Philpot grabbed Priscilla's arm as she was about to leave the room, placing the sovereign, he had lent her at the beginning of the game, to be used as a counter, before Norton had supplied wooden ones, into her hand, closing her fingers around it.

"Please keep it as a memento of a

very pleasant evening. And I thought this was going to be such a dull affair, until a very resourceful young lady made a suggestion," laughing down at her. "How wrong I was! Mother had great difficulty in making me attend this ball, because we are way-back relations of Edward's. How I objected! Thank you, Priscilla. The evening has been great fun and I would also like to write to you, if I may? You've been a breath of fresh air!"

She nodded, her eyes dancing mischievously. "But I'm not allowed to receive letters from anyone who is not my family."

"I have a sister who attends the same school as you do. Easy! *Au revoir*, young Priscilla," and with a wave of the hand, was gone.

Priscilla delighted, carefully placed the coin in her reticule. She would keep it forever.

Louise sank back on the coach seat, with a contented sigh. "I think everything went off very well, indeed,

Bertram. I hope you weren't too bored, my love?"

"No, no, I had spent a very pleasant evening in the card room, several old friends there to keep me company," he murmured sleepily.

Louise nodded to add enviously. "Wasn't the decor beautiful? A perfect foil for the many hues of the ladies' dresses. We could never have produced such magnificence," and Bertram had to agree with her.

★ ★ ★

Later that night, tired as she was, Sarah reviewed the evening, sitting up amongst her pillows. The deed was done, one that she had vowed never to do, that of becoming engaged to a man whom she did not love. Not that Edward was unacceptable. After all, he was the Earl of Weston, but that was not the reason why she had given her consent, but to get away from Louise, who was making her life a misery, plus the fact that her brother had decreed that Edward would make a kind husband and for that, she should be grateful. At least, the Countess was a dear and that Stranger?

She fingered her lips. How sweet and loving a kiss could be and the Stranger had said he had fallen in love with her, burrowing deeper into her pillows, her eyes becoming heavy. How her pulses had jumped, but smiled at this foolishness. After all, she would never see him again and Edward must never know, it would be too unkind. Suddenly, she jerked awake. Had it all been a hallucination, born of her fear of a loveless marriage? Perhaps the Stranger had had too much to drink, or taken on a silly wager? She yawned and finally fell into an exhausted sleep.

The betrothal party was given a front page splash in all the morning newspapers, hailed as the best of the Season to date. One reporter, who no doubt, must have climbed out of his bed on the wrong side, acidly wrote that he presumed Mrs. Danbury was now in high alt, at the prospect of her sister-in-law launching her two daughters on to the ton, but the rest of the dailies wrote only flowery commonplace, the Morning Standard amongst them.

Louise, with a pleased smirk, brought in the paper, reading its contents at the breakfast table, but nobody was interested, as they tried to keep their eyes open.

The next few weeks were busy ones, as Sarah was fitted out for the position she would hold, as the Earl of Weston's bride, thankful that Edward took her out driving most afternoons.

"You're looking fagged to death, dear girl," he said, one afternoon, with a quick glance, before picking up the reins. "I insist that you spend tomorrow with my mother."

Sarah was surprised and pleased, at this thoughtful suggestion. "Thank you, I'd like that, although I can't promise not to fall asleep. All the clothes that are being made for me are beautiful, the best I've ever owned, since my mother died, but with all the fittings, I'm too tired even to take the faintest interest."

"You will, once we are married," came the bracing reply, "as you swan around the neighbourhood and meeting the numerous ladies who will be making bride calls."

Sarah shuddered. "Will you be there, Edward?" she asked anxiously.

"Heavens, no!" backing away with a horrified expression. "All you will need to do is look beautiful and demure and you're more than capable of doing that, but Mother will be there, of course."

He really did have a most delightful smile, she thought, a little surprised.

Edward continued, as he feathered a corner neatly. "I have a feeling you're not a meek and mild small mouse and I'm really looking forward to getting to know you, better, Sarah," casting her a kindly glance.

The following morning a carriage was sent around to convey Sarah to the

Earl's home, the Countess welcoming her warmly, but on seeing her wan face, rang the bell.

"You are going to bed for a few hours, my dear. You look absolutely exhausted. I suppose that nip-cheese of a sister-in-law of yours, has not called in the best dressmakers, who need only to take a few measurements, discuss fabrics and patterns and the deed is done."

Sarah nodded. "It's all the standing," she confessed. "And thank you Ma'am, if it's not too much trouble."

"I have a dear friend coming this morning, so off you go, dear child. Martha will take you upstairs. She was my right hand when I came to Weston Hall, as a young bride. She'll see to your needs."

Sarah went, very willing, with this dumpy little woman with a kindly face, who had seen to their needs on the night of the ball, thankful for her supporting arm.

The bedroom to which she was taken,

was charmingly furnished, with a frilled dressing table, the curtains matching, her feet sinking into the thick pile of the floral carpet.

Martha helped her to undress, handing her a silk nightgown, that had to be one of the Countess', it was so voluminous and they both giggled.

"Now drink up your tea, Miss Sarah," said Martha quietly, fussing around seeing that her charge was comfortable, before closing the door.

Sarah woke hours later, much refreshed, to look around her idly, her mind going back to the ball and that kiss. Strange, it must have been a dream and turned over again, this time to be woken by Martha, saying that luncheon was served downstairs, helping Sarah to dress and doing her hair for her, uttering sympathetic little noises as she did so.

"You remind me of my old nurse Martha and I'm usually not so lazy," enjoying all the attention.

"So I believe, Miss, and Madam has

given orders that I train a young maid for your personal use and welcome into the family," with a gentle smile. "And now, Miss Sarah, I'll take you down to her ladyship."

Sarah felt refreshed after luncheon of spring soup, fried filleted sole, to end with a compote of apricots and cream.

"Well, I'm pleased to see you have a healthy appetite," her hostess remarked, with a satisfied nod. "Some young ladies go on a diet of vinegar and boiled potatoes. Such nonsense! No woman should look willowy," glancing down at her ample proportions.

Sarah smiled and accepted another serving of dessert.

"My dear, please tell me about your parents. I knew your mother a long time ago and see in you, a vague resemblance."

"My parents were devoted to each other and I'll never forget the way my mother took farewell of Father; he was conscious to the minute of his passing.

It was a promise that they'd meet again in God's kingdom, a tender kiss and Mother closed his eyes. Some years later, Mother died in her sleep, a smile on her lips. That's the kind of love I desire, Ma'am."

The Countess was touched. "Love will come, if you let it, my dear," to look up, as the door opened and Edward entered, to help himself to a cup of tea, greeting Sarah with a smile, but quickly excused himself, as he had matters, outside, to attend to.

Sarah rose with determination. "May I go with you, Edward?" who was startled at this request. "I'd like to share all aspects of your life and I might as well start now," biting back a smile.

The Countess chuckled at her son's expression, pleased that Sarah was no namby pamby Miss. They would deal famously together. This daughter-in-law wouldn't allow Edward to have all his own way.

"Very well, my dear, an excellent

idea. You'll need a hat," was his prosaic reply.

The days passed swiftly, Sarah and the Earl's wedding now only a few weeks away.

At times, Sarah was uneasily aware that she was making too much of the Stranger's behaviour. It could only have been a joke and she was a silly chit of a girl, to think otherwise.

This particular day had started quite normally, Bertram leaving for the office, Louise chevying the maids, Eunice happy at the prospect of a visit to a friend and Priscilla pleased that she was still on holiday.

Later that morning, Louise called for the carriage to be brought around, Sarah and Eunice setting off, Eunice to be dropped at her friend's house, while Sarah went on to Bond Street, to buy more embroidery thread, to finish a cloth she was making for her trousseau. The afternoon was just as normal, Louise taking Eunice, to call on Madame Theresa for a new gown for the wedding, arriving back to find the house in an uproar.

Sarah had been summoned earlier, by the butler, to say that the master was home early. "Miss Sarah, something dreadful must have happened," showing intense concern. "The master wants you, better go quickly."

She had hurried into the drawing-room, where her brother was seated, looking uncommonly grave. She gave him a worried glance, but said quietly, "Bertram, you've had bad news? You look ghastly," to add, trying to lift that agonized expression on his face. "Lost your fortune on 'change?" knowing immediately that that was a stupid remark to have made, regretting it immediately.

He shook his head. "Edward was killed while out fox hunting this morning."

She turned white and gripped the arms of the chair. "Oh," she gasped, horror in her voice and in her eyes. "Oh, the poor Countess!" her vague sense of relief, overpowered by her grief for that dear lady.

It was then that the rest of the family arrived, Louise and Eunice, rushing into the room, followed closely by Priscilla, to find Sarah already there. Louise sank down next to her husband, shaking his arm.

"What has occurred, to make you look like this?" she demanded. "And Sarah looks as if she's about to faint."

Bertram, his eyes haunted, his expression drained, replied hoarsely, "I was asked to call on Lady Weston, this afternoon," he gulped. "Edward is dead!"

3

FOR a moment, a heavy silence fell in the spacious drawing-room, that had suddenly appeared to have turned cold and dreary, the ticking of the clock the only sound heard.

It was Louise who broke the silence, her voice shrill with shock, as she fell back on to the cushions. "But — but how?" she spluttered. "How could this dreadful thing have happened?" her hand going to her heart.

Bertram seemed to have aged, considerably. "Evidently, he was thrown from his horse, at a rasper and broke his neck," turning his head from side to side, trying to shake the numbness from his brain.

Sarah, her face, from which all colour had ebbed, her eyes blank with disbelief, stared at her brother, her thoughts for dear Lady Weston, her grief for Edward's mother at the loss of her beloved son, her only child.

Bertram's thoughts were otherwise. Now he would again be importuned by his wife to again try and make other arrangements for Sarah. Edward's death was a bitter pill.

And Eunice, shocked and sullen. "Now I won't be able to have my come out ball, at that lovely mansion in St. James' Square!" and fled from the room, banging the door, in tearful rage and frustration.

When Louise had recovered a little from the initial shock, could only utter, "What a dreadful catastrophe! It was just as well you had not yet handed over Sarah's dowry," with sour satisfaction.

Bertram winced at this mercenary remark to say coldly, "It would have been paid back."

Sarah rose to her feet, excusing herself, unable to bear any more of Louise' mouthings, but before she could reach the door, Louise said sourly,

"Sarah, you cannot expect Bertram to arrange another such excellent match. We have to think of our own girls, now," crying out in angry disappointment, "I had such high hopes, only to have them dashed down!"

Sarah did not reply, but quietly closed the door, to find Lenten, Mrs. Smeeth and Annie, the tweeny, waiting for her, Mrs. Smeeth gathering her into her plumpness. "There, there my dearie, the Lord gives and he takes away. We all love you and are very upset by what as happened," taking Sarah upstairs, to leave her with Priscilla, who had quickly followed Sarah from the room. She hugged her, no words necessary. It was only after some time, that the companionable silence was broken by Priscilla, who, for once, was unnaturally subdued.

"What will you do now, Auntie dear?" but Sarah could only shake her head, still too upset to plan or even think lucidly, all thoughts suspended.

For several days, the whole family were still in shock, grateful that they did not have to attend Edward's funeral, which was to be a private one, at the family's country home, but it was not long before Louise adopted her old attitude, Sarah finding herself again Cinderella.

"We've gone to considerable expense on your behalf, Sarah and now this had to happen. I can't have a girl of your age, sitting around like you've been doing these last few months, when there is all that extra work to be done, as we've the Ritfords coming to dine this evening. The flowers have not yet been arranged, or the silver cleaned and I've a splitting headache, that even a feather could drop me down in this sultry weather. And now I have you to worry about," with an exaggerated sigh.

"I'm only having a cup of tea," replied Sarah reasonably, "and you won't have to worry about me, much longer. I'll soon be taking up a nursing career."

"Nursing? Pish! You're only saying that to annoy me," Louise muttered pettishly. "I'm not really well enough to bear with your flights of fancy."

Sarah shook her head firmly. "I want to become one of Florence Nightingale's nurses," her voice determined.

"Ha, a gently bred girl like you? And what will your brother say to that, Miss?"

Sarah inclined her head and did not reply, except to say that she had to water the plants in the conservatory and that everything would be done on time.

As she rose from her chair, Mrs. Smeeth laid a kindly hand on her shoulder. "Finish your tea, Miss Sarah. There's no need to be in a tizz. You know what the Mistress is like, when she is expecting friends to dine," she whispered, with a wary eye on Louise. The housekeeper thought it a shame the way Miss Sarah was treated, so unnecessary, too.

Sarah, however, did take the liberty

to visit the Countess one afternoon. She had told Louise of her plans, and had added, "I'm not sad for myself, but my heart goes out to that grand old lady and she was so looking forward to being the Dowager Countess."

Louise had brightened. "I think it would be an excellent idea if you fostered that friendship, Sarah and you may take the carriage," she had said, handsomely. "It would be dreadful if you arrived in a hack. I expect too, that the heir will soon be taking up his new position. Perhaps, he's not married," and Sarah had left her with much to think about.

The house had a special ambience about it, as Sarah entered it and felt that she was welcome beneath its portals.

She was ushered into the Countess' private sittingroom by the butler, who said with a kindly smile, "You'll be a ray of sunshine to my lady," he murmured with deep feeling.

Sarah was given a warm greeting, but she noticed sadly, the deep shadows under her hostess' eyes.

"Ma'am, I'm not intruding, am I? Please tell me so, if I am, but I felt I had to come and see you to say how sorry I am at your tragic loss. Words are so inadequate, aren't they?"

The Countess had risen, Sarah putting her arms around the old lady.

"What a sweet child you are, dear, to think of me and you're most welcome. I did so want you to be Edward's bride," returning the embrace, "and the mother of my grandchildren." She broke down then, Sarah comforting her. "They brought him home on a gate," she murmured brokenly, into Sarah's shoulder. "Oh, my dear!" but drew away, to wipe her eyes. "There are times in one's life, when one must fight events alone, but Sarah, whenever you can spare the time, please come and see me, I'd like to keep in touch with you," and Sarah gave her promise.

"Now come and sit down and I'll ring for the teatray," with a quivering lip.

A maid entered and poured the tea, also offering small, sweet biscuits. Sarah said, when the silence had become a little oppressive, "I had a very high regard for your son, but it just wasn't meant to be," she said sadly.

What a dreadful shock and dreams broken, this catastrophe had been for this dear person, whom she had been learning to love and appreciate, blinking away these thoughts and was comforted when the Countess said again, that she hoped Sarah would continue to visit her, not willing to cut the thread that bound them together.

Lady Weston was sitting up straighter. "I belong to a soldiering family and death was something we had to face. I lost two of my uncles in the wars," to lapse into a remembering silence and it was only when Sarah filled her cup again, that she continued, "I have always regretted that I was unable to give my husband any more children. Now this had to happen."

Thinking to change the subject, Sarah began telling the Countess about her dream of becoming a nurse and hurriedly explained when she saw Lady Weston's surprise.

"Even before Bertram had made that marriage arrangement with your son, I had spoken to my brother about this. Naturally, he was very upset, but has always realised that Louise and I have never seen eye to eye."

"Would you be able to face the dreadful sights, a gently reared girl, like you?"

"Florence Nightingale was also gently reared," Sarah reminded her, "and has reached the heights of her career, revolutionising the nursing and hospital services."

"Especially the plight of our soldiers," added the Countess, nodding her head, in agreement.

"Soon I will visit the hospital and apply to join and to find out if they will take me," Sarah said, with a cheerful grin.

"I suppose Louise is making life hard for you again, Sarah?" who nodded.

"I've longed to join the nursing profession, ever since I learnt about that great lady and her work," and was surprised when her hostess rang the bell and asked Martha to find the file, holding newspaper clippings, Martha greeting Sarah kindly, before going off.

While they were waiting, Sarah opened her purse and took out her engagement ring and diamond necklace, handing them over to the Countess, who took them with a sad smile.

"The heir, who I haven't seen for years, will take possession of these," laying the heirlooms on the small side table next to her.

It was a relief when Martha returned with the file, both ladies looking through the cuttings, Lady Weston putting aside her sorrow, Sarah remarking, "What a hoarder of newspaper cuttings, you are, Ma'am."

"Well, it is history in the making.

What a superb lady Florence Nightingale is," murmured Lady Weston.

"And what a change there has been! Oh, look here a press cutting about the Crimean war and the public outcry about the deplorable hospital conditions there and how she revolutionized the army's hospital services. Ma'am, I'm so pleased you have kept these. How interesting!"

"I have here a report that she also looked into the sanitary conditions, existing in our army camps in India. I'd forgotten that! Ah, here's a report about the starting of a training school for nurses at St. Thomas', Sarah. That should interest you," handing over the cutting and silence fell for a while.

"My dear, you will let me know all your news?" Lady Weston asked anxiously.

"Indeed I will, for I expect it will only be Priscilla, bless her, who will be at all interested," with a sudden rush of pleasure, brightening her countenance.

Louise met Sarah on her return,

Lenten hovering in the background, shaking his grey head sadly. The mistress was in a foul temper again.

"Where have you been, Miss, might I ask?"

Sarah told her quietly, slipping off her blue redingote, placing it carefully over a chair. "Louise you knew I was to visit the Countess and even suggested I keep in contact with her. Why the sudden change?"

"Oh, I still agree, of course, but need you have stayed so long?" her tone brittle.

"Yes," replied Sarah firmly, "for Lady Weston brought out all her newspaper cuttings, referring to Florence Nightingale, which I found of interest naturally and she sends her kindest regards."

Louise was mollified, her voice softening, somewhat. "Well, I hope you don't expect Mary to take your coat upstairs and help is needed in the kitchen. One of the maids is off sick. Please go immediately."

Sarah held a tight rein on her tongue, replying that soon she would be no longer a burden.

"What are you about to do?" demanded her sister-in-law in alarm, but this question fell on deaf ears, for Sarah had disappeared into the nether regions, wondering how her brother had ever come to marry this woman, but had to admit fairly, that Louise was a different creature when her husband was at home and at these times it was a haven of peace in otherwise troubled days.

Sarah sank gratefully, into bed that night, determined that she would have to do something about her situation and soon. Not surprisingly, her dreams were troubled, but in the early morning awoke to drowsily think about the Stranger. It was silly to think that he would call on her. It was like wishing for the moon, but the thought persisted. Surely, by now, he must have read about Edward's demise in the papers. Would he seek her out and what would her reaction be, she wondered idly.

No other man had ever taken her in his arms, other than her father, which had never been nerve-shaking, whereas the Stranger's embrace had been and that kiss? Had she returned it? She couldn't remember for she had been too taken aback. Now the memory was a warm blanket of comfort that she needed so badly and fell into a deep, peaceful sleep, to be awoken by Mrs. Smeeth opening the door, bringing in a ewer of hot water and drawing back the curtains, to flood the room with bright sunshine, whilst giving her a cheery "good morning".

"It's a lovely day, dear," noticing Sarah's happy expression. "Better wash quickly, lovey, the water aint all that hot," pouring it into the basin and setting out a towel.

Sarah stretched, luxuriously. "It certainly is, Mrs. Smeeth," swinging her legs out of the bed, her toes feeling for her slippers.

"I'm that pleased, Miss Sarah dear, to see 'ow 'appy you are this morning. The Mistress was certainly out of sorts, yesterday, but then we all know why," tapping the side of her nose, suggestively. "I suppose we must excuse her, for the mistress had such 'igh 'opes."

Sarah cut in quickly, with an impish smile. "From this day onwards, Smeethie, I'm going to take control of my life," to add even more firmly. "No more arrangements are going to be made for me."

"And how might you do that, my dearie," hands on hips, but the question was anxious. No one knew, better than she, what Miss Sarah had had to put up with over the years.

"I'm going to visit the hospital and offer myself as a nurse," she ended up triumphantly.

The good woman's mouth dropped. "Never, Miss Sarah!" she breathed. "Not that I say it aint a bad idea, so good luck I says, because the Mistress does not play fair by you, making you nothing but a drudge, not that me and the maids don't appreciate what you do. Lenten will miss you," and with that parting shot, the housekeeper closed the door, allowing Sarah to quickly wash and dress. No maid for her, she thought cynically, as she brushed out her curly hair, tying it into a severe bun at the back of her neck. She was ready to go downstairs.

As the days passed, she began to draw more and more comfort from the memory of the Stranger and from the fact that there was someone out there, who loved her, filling her with a nameless, intangible pleasure, his face coming between her and the work she had to do, as Louise vented her disappointment on her head, until it became unbearable.

Would Bertram, this time, give his permission for her to join the nursing profession? If not she was determined to take the matters in her own hands, a wry smile creasing her lips, remembering the time she had marched into his office and the outcome. Now Edward was dead and she was about to talk to Bertram again about this matter. This did much to help her through the day, Louise, as usual difficult.

That evening when all the family were in the drawing room, she again asked her brother if she could join the staff at St. Thomas', pleasantly surprised and relieved at his first words.

"I've been expecting this question, my dear and I cannot hold you back from what you feel you must do, or stand in your way. After all, we are all aware that our dear Florence Nightingale is a gently reared woman who has risen to great heights in her effort to alleviate the plight of, not only our wounded soldiers, but also other sick folk. You have my blessing and what a resourceful girl, you are! I'm proud of you," with a beam.

Sarah rushed to him to give him a hug. "You are a dear, Bertram and thank you."

Bertram, however, had something else to add, saying with concern, "You must realise, Sarah, that if you are successful in becoming a nurse, this would in all intents and purposes, renounce any respectable offers of marriage?"

Louise had been silent, aghast at this latest plan. "Sarah, I had no idea that you were serious. I — I thought you were only teasing me when you spoke about this several days ago. What will people think?"

"And what are my friends going to say, when they hear of this silly plan of yours?" muttered Eunice, with a reproachful glare at her father. "It's absurd!" she added heatedly.

"I think it's a wonderful idea and after all, Auntie will be living a life of her own choosing," Priscilla cut in belligerently, her soft mouth firming. "And Papa, I hope you don't make any marriage arrangements for me. I also want to love the man I marry," and ran from the room, overhearing her mother's remark.

"Now see what you have done, Bertram! Upset us all!"

"Nonsense!" retorted her husband, who was, nevertheless, a trifle upset by his family's reaction, turned to his sister. "Sarah, Louise and I both hope you'll visit us from time to time. We don't want tongues to wag more than necessary, but would like to know how you go on," to which Sarah was only too happy to agree, thankful for the successful outcome of her plans.

"Please don't worry about me, Bertie," with a warm rush of emotion, "but I'm determined to go and visit the recruiting officer at the hospital soon and will keep you all informed," her emerald green eyes sparkling, as they hadn't done for some time.

Bertram listened quietly, relief flickering behind his hazel eyes, but very conscious that, in some way, he had failed this beloved sister of his.

Sarah excused herself, gleefully confident that the next hurdle would be easy, but leaving her brother with twin parallel lines, across his usually placid brow. In all their years together since childhood, he had never realised what a stubborn streak this sister of his had, reminding him strongly of his father. Sarah had spunk! Other women of his acquaintance, would have railed at the blow fate had decreed for Sarah, but she had uttered no word of bitterness, his ego not allowing the fact that she was only too thankful she would not have to be a partner in a loveless marriage.

The following morning the story was out, presumably Mrs. Smeeth had talked. Louise was livid!

"Sarah, you are going to have to work extremely hard, for a mere pittance," she reminded her with a sneer.

She could not stop herself from saying quietly, "But I do that here, Louise," determined that she would visit the hospital that very afternoon.

Her sister-in-law had coloured up, looking a little disconcerted, although inwardly thankful that her thorn in the flesh would soon be gone, but was left to wonder again, uneasily, what society would say, about this latest quirk. No doubt she would get the blame, were her bitter thoughts.

Priscilla had been all ears, during the morning, but refrained from any comment. Sarah was kept busy, so she had no time for a chat, but later asked her mother if she could go shopping with Sarah, as she needed several items for school, when it started again. Louise giving her consent.

After luncheon, Sarah rushed to her room, quickly changing into a blue sprigged muslin frock and a small straw hat, her eyes laughing back at her from the mirror, at the thought of her coming interview with the recruiting officer at the hospital.

She was ready when Priscilla popped her head around the door, in a pretty pale pink outfit, her fair hair escaping from under her wide-brimmed hat, saying she was going to enjoy the afternoon of shopping, with a cheeky grin.

Sarah nodded, with a twitching lip at the way her niece had obtained the carriage and in the most unprincipled way, too, giving her an exuberant hug. "You're the most redoubtable girl! Going shopping, forsooth!"

"Think nothing of it, Auntie mine," Priscilla replied handsomely. "I'm sure I've inherited some of your traits. You are indeed intrepid, looking for a nursing position. Perhaps I'll join you one day, your rebellion paving the way for me? I'm certainly not willing to sit at home waiting for Papa to make marriage arrangement for me. I rather like Kim Philpot," she confided and at Sarah's raised eyebrows added demurely, "I have met his sister, Dora, a very nice person and shall keep up the friendship. Remember, I told you that she goes to the same school as I do?"

"Priscilla, have you met Mr. Philpot again?" eyeing her niece with some concern.

"Oh, yes," airily, "and he again promised he'd write to me," leaving Sarah shaking her head.

Their carriage was waiting patiently for them and soon they were bowling down the street, Priscilla remarking smugly that this was far more pleasant than having to hail a hack. "Which you would have had to do, Sarah, but I really do need to purchase a few things."

"We'll do your shopping first, love and on the way back, we'll call in at St. Thomas'."

They spent a pleasant half hour in town, going through Priscilla's list, to return to the carriage and were driven to the hospital.

It was only then that Sarah said in alarm, "Oh, dear! Do you think I should have worn my navy skirt and jacket?"

"Too late!" exclaimed Priscilla dramatically. "Your very presence and laying your hand on fevered brows, will instantly heal every male you nurse!"

"I'll have to wear a uniform," retorted her aunt, repressively.

Her heartbeat increased as they approached St. Thomas', gazing up at the impressive pile, her whole being filled with a passionate hope that she would be accepted as a nurse, to have a deep committment, but must face the fact that she might not be accepted, her background too refined. Mrs. Nightingale had an exceptionally fine background, she argued and hope was again born. Another disturbing thought came to mind. She would have to nurse men, see them unclothed. Once again the great lady came to her aid. She had had to, she reminded herself, hardily.

Sarah was brought back to reality by Priscilla, asking her if she might accompany her to the interview.

"Of course," she replied. "You're my chaperone," which produced a chuckle from her niece.

"I feel very grownup and a little awed by the occasion," she confessed, as they walked up the steps with light feet, Priscilla keeping close, wrinkling her small, upturned nose, at the strong smell that pervaded the entrance hall.

A nurse arrived and kindly showed them into a waitingroom. "What a dowdy uniform," whispered Priscilla. "I'll want a frilly one," a remark which Sarah ignored.

The lady who interviewed Sarah, was a Miss Hilda Norbury, rather thin, with a commanding air about her.

Being a rather plain person herself and not ever having had an offer of marriage, she was surprised that such a beautiful girl should want to take up nursing. With that creamy skin, tawny hair and those greeny eyes, one would have thought that young men would have fallen over themselves, to court her. She sighed. To the patients, this girl would be an angel of light.

"Miss Danbury, may I ask you the reasons why you would like to nurse?" her brown eyes keen.

It was Priscilla who replied. "Sarah is not comfortable at home," Sarah silencing her, by placing a hand on her knee, to add,

"I don't get on very well with my sister-in-law."

Miss Norbury nodded, understanding the situation to continue with the list of questions that had to be answered and at the end, surprised Sarah by saying a little diffidently, but her glance speculative.

"Miss Danbury, I know what I'm about to ask, is a little unorthodox, but I have a very dear friend, not connected with this hospital, who is very anxious to hire a companion, who will also help look after her nine year old son, a very lively youngster. Mrs. Merton is due to sail back to Hong Kong and is desperate to find the right person to accompany her. I feel that you might suit her, that is, if you so desire?"

An excited exclamation broke from Priscilla, Sarah once again having to silence her, with a quick touch.

Miss Norbury smiled sympathetically,

before continuing, "Mrs. Merton is a charming person, but needs support. Lachrymose, is how I would describe her, but very kind," she hastened to add.

Sarah nodded, eyes bright, her smile wide. What a wonderful opportunity to travel. "Miss Norbury, may I give you an answer after I have met this lady?"

"Of course and would you mind visiting her now, Miss Danbury? As I've said this matter is of some urgency and I'm sure she will be in, as she hasn't been very well," busily writing a note and giving the address to Sarah. "I do hope you get this position and when you return," smiling kindly, "your application will be most favourably considered. Thank you most sincerely and by the way, Mrs. Merton is a friend of the family."

"Well!" exclaimed Priscilla, as they retraced their steps to the carriage. "Hong Kong, where's that? I was dying to ask, but didn't like to show my ignorance."

"We'll soon find out," murmured her aunt, as she gave John Coachman the directions, adding that he need not wait, as they did not know how long they would be. "We'll take a hack home, John."

The old man nodded. "Miss Priscilla whispered to me that you are after a position. Good luck, Miss Sarah and I'll say naught back home," patting the side of his nose, his rheumy old eyes twinkling, Sarah smiling her thanks.

Even before the ladies had settled themselves, Priscilla said excitedly, "Oh, Auntie dear, I do hope you'll get this position and meet someone really nice. It's going to be so romantic, the sea and the sun and all that and if you don't meet anyone you fancy going over, there will be the return trip," throwing her arms wide, to sober quickly. "I'm going to miss you so much and — and after this mishap, will you want to get married?" she asked curiously.

Sarah nodded soberly. "But I'll not

have your father make any more plans for me. Perhaps gentlemen will feel that some bad luck is connected with me?"

Her niece burst out laughing. "If that is what's in your cockloft — "

Sarah's shocked face stopped her. "Ladies do not use that kind of language," she said sternly.

Priscilla begged pardon demurely, hiding her telltale eyes, twiddling her thumbs.

Sarah smiled, shaking her head. "Priscilla, I would like to marry the right man," thinking again of the Stranger. Why had he not called? Was it too soon?

The carriage was slowing down, Sarah turning to Priscilla. "Dear, please delay any remarks you may feel you have to make, until we leave. Please!"

Her niece's one fault was that she could not hold her too candid tongue, words that were blurted out, without due, or kindly thought. Very often the family were put to the blush, by her

123

forthright comments.

They were met by a sprightly butler and were shown into the front parlour that was tastefully furnished and where a sweet lady was sitting who rose at their entrance. She brightened considerably, when Sarah told her that she had been asked by Miss Norbury at the hospital to visit her.

"I believe you need a companion, Mrs. Merton," said Sarah kindly, handing her the note.

"Oh, how very obliging of Miss Norbury! Such a dear person! Have you come to apply for the post and would you be prepared to come with me and my young son to Hong Kong?" Her whole manner had brightened, but her tone was still anxious.

Sarah and Priscilla nodded, Sarah to say with a beam, "I'd love to accompany you, Ma'am, if you think I'll be able to fill the position satisfactorily?"

"My dear, I think you'll be ideal and who's this other young lady?" holding out her hand.

"I'm Priscilla, Mrs. Merton, Sarah's niece," bobbing a curtsy. "I'm her chaperone for today, so she says."

"And very nice, too," Mrs. Merton returning the happy smile. "Now, shall we get down to business, Miss Danbury."

"Oh, please call me, Sarah," with a happy nod.

Mrs. Merton liked the poise of this young woman and the fleeting shy smile, pleased her. Harry would definitely like her, she decided happily. Her problem had been solved, thanks to Hilda Norbray.

Mrs. Merton smiled, wondering why this gently bred girl was in need of employment, but it was not her business to pry. Instead she asked if they both would like some tea.

It was Priscilla who replied, saying that they were both parched, as they had been in town for some time and was quite happy to pull the embroidered bell rope, admiring it as she did so.

The two elder ladies got down to

business, Mrs. Merton stating salary, naming a figure that made Sarah's face glow. "All your expenses will be paid, of course, including a return ticket," Sarah so overcome, she could not reply, except to nod.

The tea arrived, Priscilla drinking hers quickly, in a most unladylike manner and accepted a second cup.

Seeing Sarah's scandalized face, Mrs. Merton chose to be amused, saying that she was quite used to young people, having two of her own and added, "I'm in need of a bright spirit, as the journey is a long one and I'm not a good traveller. I came over to bring my eldest son, so that he could start the new year at Eton. Naturally, we are going to miss him, sorely," trying to control her quivering mouth. "This is my brother's house and he and my sister-in-law, will keep an eye on him and invite him home for the short holidays. My youngest son will be going back with me. Harry is only nine, a very active young man, so I'll need your help there, too. I do hope you'll come back with us," with almost a pleading smile.

"Mrs. Merton, may I ask when you will be leaving? I was led to believe that it was soon."

"My dear, on Monday and that is why I have been so distracted. Will you manage to be ready in such a short space of time?" and when Sarah nodded, heaved a sigh of relief. "Please be here by 1 o'clock. We've got to catch the boat-train that will take us to Southampton. The boat sails at 4 p.m." She rose to her feet, "Now, my dears, I'll order the carriage to take you home. Goodbye and thank you, Sarah," holding her hand in both of hers. "Fletcher will see you out."

As they climbed into the comfortable carriage, it was to find it had another occupant, a dear little short haired terrier, with the most intelligent brown eyes and one ear cocked. He sat perfectly still in his corner, his thumping tail, his only movement.

Priscilla fell in love with him, immediately.

"Hope you don't mind, Miss, travelling with a dog. He'll not bother you and stays in his own corner, but if you don't like it, please say and I'll turn 'im out," said the coachman, "and I'll have 'im up with me."

"Oh, please don't! He's such a dear little thing, so well behaved," said Priscilla, holding out a tentative hand, which the little animal nuzzled. "He must like carriage rides."

"Miss, like all of us, he craves company. I picked him up, one day, a thin, miserable scrap — "

"What's his name?" she asked eagerly, her blue eyes alight. "Do you think I might have him for my very own?" Her face fell. "I go back to school soon and nobody else would look after him, but it would only be for another year — " her eyes pleaded.

"He's name is Rex, Miss and I can't remember when I last met such a bright little lady. What would you think about the idea of you looking after 'im, and he's taken to you, look how close he's sitting, while you're on holiday and I'll look after 'im while you're at school?"

"Oh, Sarah," turning sparkling eyes to her, "do you think Mother would mind?" fondling the dog's head as it lay on her lap.

"It's not for me to say, dear, you must ask your father first. He's never unreasonable."

"Well Miss, now that is settled, I'll be driving you home," asking for the directions. "Now the family will be interested in this address," he added. "And a very nice area it is too, Miss."

"But why — " asked Sarah, not quite understanding. "Oh, I see! Yes, Mrs. Merton could be taking a cuckoo into the nest," and watched his craggy face break into a wry grin, showing several blackened teeth.

"Just so, Miss. One can't be too careful these days, but it weren't Mrs. Merton wot was worried, but her sister, in case Mrs. Merton had not given any thought as to your background, Miss. It were Maggie, who brought you in your tea, who heard you was to go with Mrs. Merton to Hong Kong and told the mistress. Hope that is no offence to you?" a little anxiously.

Sarah hastened to assure him, as he closed the door and they were driven away.

She glanced across at Priscilla who was totally absorbed, as she whispered to the little dog. Here was a solution that could go far in giving Priscilla companionship for at least a week, before she started school, her niece turning to her as she became conscious of her concern.

"I'm going to miss you dreadfully," her full bottom lip wobbling, her eyes filming. "Home won't be the same without you, Auntie, we're kindred spirits. Eunice is Mother's favourite and Father is always in his study."

Sarah seeing her distress, gathered her close. "But never too busy to listen to you. Dear, won't you talk to him more often? I think you'll be agreeably surprised," pleased when Priscilla nodded, "And when I return to begin my nursing career, we'll see each other in the holidays. We'll stroll in the park and look at the shops, while you tell me your news and I'll tell you mine," to add, "Mrs. Merton really does need someone to accompany her and to look after her son." Sarah knew she was gabbling, but could not bear to see Priscilla so upset.

"And perhaps your Father will allow you to keep this dear little dog," she suggested brightly.

As they drew up at the house, Priscilla couldn't scramble out quick enough, as the old coachman helped them down.

"Now, Missie," he said quietly, "don't you fret. Old Joe won't be throwing that little 'un back into the alleyways and what about going in and asking your pa and ma, if you might keep 'im? I'll wait."

It was Sarah who replied. "Thank

131

you for that suggestion, but it won't do. I've been very remiss and should have asked Mrs. Merton if my brother could visit her this evening. Both families then, I hope, will be saved some anxiety. I will ask my brother, as soon as he has returned home, if he will visit Mrs. Merton this evening. We'll then give you an answer about the little dog."

As he nodded his grey head, she added, "Please give Mrs. Merton this message and if she has another engagement, would you mind coming back and telling me so?"

Joe was very willing to do this. "Leave it to me, Missie," as he scrambled up onto his seat, Rex already there, his tongue hanging out.

As Sarah entered the hall, she was met by an anxious Priscilla. "Mother says I must ask Father. Oh Sarah! I hope he says yes."

"We will just have to have a little patience. Not long now," with a glance at the grandfather clock, that had been in her home, in her youth. "There he is now," but her words fell on deaf ears for Priscilla had picked up her skirts and flew down the steps, to meet her father, coming back, looking a little more cheerful.

"Papa wants to know all," she whispered dramatically.

Sarah told her news to the rest of the family at tea that afternoon.

"Hong Kong!" exclaimed Bertram, his mouth dropping, his eyes bulging, "but — but I thought you wanted to go nursing," he said, completely bewildered.

Louise after the initial surprise, said calmly that Sarah would certainly see a little more of the world, while Eunice, as usual, was frankly envious, saying she would give her back teeth to be going.

"And this Mrs. Merton? What kind of a woman is she?" her brother wanted to know.

Priscilla had been strangely quiet, but this was too much for her and explained eagerly.

"Mrs. Merton is a dear, a little on the plump side, who desperately needs a companion and also help with her nine year old son, who we did not meet." She suddenly stopped short, her guilty glance going to her aunt, who had also seen the trap.

"We?" asked her mother quickly, looking displeased. "We? I suppose you must have accompanied Sarah? I thought you said you were going shopping, Miss?"

"Only after that, Mother," murmured Priscilla soothingly, "and I promise I had nothing to say during Sarah's interview, but I felt Sarah needed some support," lowering her eyes, to add primly, "Mother, it is not every day that ladies of our class have to look for employment," leaving Louise disconcerted, with the feeling that she had just been reprimanded by her youngest daughter, her father chuckling.

Sarah hurriedly, tried to cover this

gaffe. "Bertram, I asked the coachman to ask Mrs. Merton, if she would see you tonight. I should have asked her myself, I'm sorry. Would you mind paying her a courtesy call? It would certainly set your mind at rest. Please! We are to leave on Monday, so this matter is urgent."

He agreed, turning to his wife, to ask her if she would also like to go, but she declined. At that moment, Lenten came in with a message from Mrs. Merton, to say that she would be in all evening and would welcome a visit from Mr. Danbury and that her carriage was at his disposal. Sarah sighed with relief. One hurdle had been cleared. Bertram left.

Some time later a maid came in to announce that dinner was ready and should she serve it, Louise replying that they would wait for the master, but at that moment, Lenten asked Priscilla to go with him and there in the hall, stood her father and old Joe, looking very pleased with themselves, beside them was the dog, who gave her an ecstatic welcome, Priscilla rushing forward to hug her father.

"You've brought Rex," laughing and crying, to dash away her tears. "Oh, thank you, Papa!"

The coachman thought it was time to depart, patting the small animal, telling him to behave himself, Priscilla wringing his hand, who was touched by this effusion.

"You're a good little soul, Prissy," said her father, "and I thought he'd be a good companion for you, while Sarah is away. Come let's go and introduce him to the rest of the family. At least, he's well behaved, which will please your mother. Now, I'm sure dinner is about to be served."

As soon as they reached the dining-room, she thanked her mother for allowing her to keep Rex, to add importantly, "He won't be any trouble, Mama, while I'm away at school for Mrs. Merton's coachman, has very kindly promised to keep him. I'll pay him, of course, out of my allowance. Now please excuse me, I must show Rex around the house and garden, for he'll have to learn how to go on in a gentleman's residence," with a show of dignity that was new to her, that made her father and Sarah smile.

Louise was just about to protest that it was dinner time, when Bertram shook his head.

"Leave the child, her dinner can be put aside until later," helping himself to lamb cutlets, fried potatoes and green beans, with a heavy hand, to add ruefully, "If I'd known what pleasure a dog could give that child, I'd have found one long ago." Only he knew what a wrench for Priscilla it was going to be when his sister left.

"I don't know what all the fuss is about," said Eunice pertly, "There is Pug and anyway, he's been badly named. Rex is the name for a large dog."

Her father damped down his retort. "But that's not the same as owning one's own pet. I well remember, when I was given my first pup and was told to train it properly." He was back in the past. "What firm friends we became."

The talk then turned to Sarah's proposed trip, Bertram saying that he had found Mrs. Merton to be a very pleasant lady and what was more, he had remembered that her husband had been seconded to the Governor's office in Hong Kong, several years ago now. So we had a lot to chat about and I asked to be kindly remembered to William, an extremely pleasant man, so Sarah, you'll go with my blessings," smiling kindly across at her. "You should have a very pleasant trip and not too long either, now that the Suez Canal has been opened," dwelling on the happy thought that he could now approach Her Majesty's Principal Secretary of State for Foreign Affairs, and ask for a travel document for Sarah. The meeting might even bear fruit, for he would ask if there was any chance of being transferred to that department.

Excusing himself, he hurried to his study to mull over how he would approach this matter and what words he would use.

The following morning, Sarah was once again in Bertram's study.

"I'm very pleased that you will be able to visit Hong Kong," he said, to add with deep feeling, "I admire your bravery in going half way across the world," a strong shudder shaking his large frame. "I'm the world's worst traveller, as well you know. I like my feet firmly planted on mother earth." A companionable silence fell, until he said gruffly. "I'm sorry the way events have fallen. I thought I had made a perfect arrangement for you, but it was not to be."

Sarah smiled at him across the desk. "You must not blame yourself. You did the best for me and I was grateful. Anyway, who could have foreseen Edward's tragic death? Now

I'm determined to make my own way in life and dear Mrs. Merton has made it possible and when I arrive back, I have the promise of a nursing career. I'm thrilled, Bertie! I really am," seeing his worried frown, ignoring his faint protest, but he knew when to bow to the inevitable and when he spoke again, it was on the subject of Hong Kong's history.

"It has been a Crown Colony since 1843, when it was annexed, from under the Chinese' noses. Two years previously the flag had been raised, Queen Victoria and Lord Palmerston very much against this latest British acquisition, both referring to it as 'just a rock'." He chuckled. "From all reports, the Colony is thriving, Arthur Kennedy now the Governor.

"You'll no doubt be writing and I for one, am looking forward, keenly, to your letters." He then went on to more personal matters. "It's very short notice, but I'm confident that I shall be able to procure travel documents for you," rising, "Time I was leaving. Goodbye, dear."

The following evening, he very proudly handed Sarah her document, Priscilla leaning over to read, "*We, Edward Henry Stanley, Earl of Derby, Baron Stanley of Bickerstaffe, a peer and a Baronet of England, a member of Her Britannic Majesty's Most Honourable Privy Council, Her Majesty's Principal Secretary of State for Foreign Affairs. Etc, Etc, Etc,.*

Request and require in the Name of Her Majesty, all those whom it may concern to allow Miss Sarah May Danbury, British subject, travelling to Hong Kong to pass freely, without let or hinderance and to afford her every assistance and protection of which she may stand in need.

Given at the Foreign Office, London the 6 day of September 1876. Signed Derby.

"You have to sign too, on the left side, Sarah," giving a huge sigh.

"What beautiful penmanship. Perhaps,

I could get a position in Father's office and write out documents. My writing is good," she said hopefully.

"Perhaps by that time, positions might be open to females," was the only comment her father made, hoping fervently, that that time would never come.

Louise pooh poohed the idea, saying that she would much rather see both daughters married.

Mrs. Smeeth and the old butler were most concerned about Sarah, both saying how much they would miss her.

"Is this Mrs. Merton a nice, kindly lady?" quavered Lenten. "Miss Sarah, I can't bear to think of you going off to the ends of the earth, to all them heathens. Not so easy to come back home, if things go wrong, now can you? Don't want you to get from the frying pan into the fire, Miss, as the saying goes."

"Please don't worry about me, you two dear people, but thank you for your concern, but I'll be fine. Mrs. Merton is a very kind lady and so is her young son," refraining from mentioning that she had yet to meet that young gentleman. "I promise I'll write to you, a long newsy letter from the first port of call, somewhere in the Mediterranean, I suppose," but neither the old butler or Mrs. Smeeth were any the wiser. "It's best I take up a position of employment," Sarah added gently.

"Aye, we understand," the two old servants replied, "but the place won't be the same without you, Miss Sarah," murmured Mrs. Smeeth, wiping her eyes on her snowy apron.

That night Sarah dreamt that the Stranger had called and had been turned away by Louise, awakening with tears streaming down her cheeks, to sit up and sternly remind herself, that Lenten would tell him where she had gone, sinking back into a peaceful sleep again.

The following afternoon, Sarah told Louise that she was going to visit the

Countess, to appraise her of her plans and also to say goodbye, Louise in agreement and offered the carriage. So Sarah donned her bonnet, shook out her sunshade and tripped her way to the mews, where their carriage was kept, to find John just about to mount the box. He reprimanded her by saying that she should have waited for him.

"Thank you, John, but it's such a lovely day, I couldn't resist it," smiling sunnily at him, as he opened the carriage door, with a flourish.

"Miss Sarah, bless you," was all he could say, muttering under his breath that it was a crying shame that Miss Sarah had to go out and work.

As he drove off, he mused on fate and this business of the high ups marrying to keep the blood line pure. Too cold blooded for his liking, but he did feel sorry for the Countess, losing her only son like that, but good luck to Miss Sarah, breaking away from convention and I'll bet all the old tabbies will have lots to say about that, as he stopped in front of the house in St. James' Square, waiting until Sarah had disappeared into the mansion.

Norton welcomed her kindly ringing a bell, Martha arriving, a smile breaking through, as she saw who the visitor was. "Miss Sarah, my lady will be that glad to see you! Come along in."

As Sarah followed Martha, the Stranger once more came to mind. Out there somewhere was the gentleman who said he had fallen in love with her across a crowded ballroom, the compulsion so great that he had put aside the codes of good behaviour, to take her in his arms, his face full of tenderness to kiss her and then to leave her in utter confusion. What were the colour of his eyes — she could not remember.

Why hadn't someone made a comment? Had the guests thought he was a relation of hers, congratulating her on her engagement?

Martha ushered her into the drawing-room, saying she would order tea, Sarah finding that it wasn't going to be an easy visit.

The Countess, who had taken her son's death, so courageously, now broke down, when Sarah told her that she would be leaving the country for a while. "My dear, I'll miss you. Oh, why did my son not heed me years ago when I pleaded that he should marry and beget an heir? Now he's dead," she ended up tearfully, dabbing her eyes with a wisp of a handkerchief.

All Sarah could do was place a comforting arm around the old lady, thankful when the teatray arrived, to suggest that she pour.

Lady Weston pulled herself together and nodded. "Please tell me where you are going and what your plans are," and Sarah told her.

"Dear, I'm pleased that you've a chance to enjoy a sea cruise and see Hong Kong. I shall certainly pay a visit to Hookham's Library and read all about that country, and will be able to talk about it sensibly."

Sarah had risen to her feet and the Countess continued. "My home will always be open to you, Sarah dear," kissing her fondly. "Strange, I have never realised what an intrepid streak you have in you."

Even Sarah had been surprised at herself, but there was also an exaltation, that she would now be allowed to run her own life and no more would she allow either Bertram or Louise to dictate her destiny.

* * *

During the last evening, Priscilla helped Sarah to pack, Rex under the bed snoring, his paws twitching, Sarah grateful that she had her trousseau to fall back on. Soon a pile of clothing lay on the bed, Sarah deciding that all she would need was there, until Priscilla took out the gown she had worn at her betrothal ball.

"You must take that," she insisted, "You never know when you might need it," who was optimistically hoping that her aunt would meet someone nice on board ship, but Sarah shook her head.

"What would I need a dress like that for? I'll be catching the next boat home and my other party gowns are quite good enough for that."

For once Priscilla did not argue as she helped pack the clothes into the trunk and a small carpet bag, Sarah eventually, sitting back on her heels, pushing a tendril away from her face.

"All that's gone in nicely, thank goodness," and was just about to close the lid, when her niece brought out the ball gown and proceeded to fold it carefully. "There is space in this trunk, Auntie mine. This will lie in the hump and will not crush at all. You've got to take it, you never know," she added cryptically. "You might even be invited to spend some time in Hong Kong, before you come back," and proceeded to close the lid, turning to Sarah with a twinkle. "Please, I have a feeling — "

"Oh, you and your feelings," muttered her aunt, conceding gracefully, unable to withstand Priscilla's wheedling tones to say, laughingly, "Prissy dear, don't ever become prim and proper!"

The following day, Mrs. Smeeth packed the last items into the bag, Priscilla noticing that Sarah had done her hair in a more severe style, which would suit her new position, she supposed, frowning fiercely. "Ah, very schoolmarmish!"

It was with a feeling of relief when Sarah, after an early luncheon, was finally helped into the carriage, by John, her luggage strapped on behind.

Priscilla had been tearful and Louise, unusually affable, presented her with a warm brown cloak with a hood saying that she might have need of it on the voyage and wished her a pleasant journey. Sarah was touched.

She leant out of the window until the carriage turned the corner sinking back against the comfortable squabs, fingering the lapel watch that Bertram had given her earlier that day. His leave taking had been emotional, as he was still suffering from a bruised spirit, that Sarah had thought to leave his home. It had upset his sense of what was right, fearing that he had failed the trust his mother had placed in him at her death, but he had not withheld his sincere blessings.

He had also given her a well-stocked purse, with a sheepish grin and had watched her face light up as she peeped into it, waving away her protests. "My dear, it is in appreciation for all you have done for us over the years and if I can, will see you at the station," which had left her with a warm sense of happiness.

Mrs. Merton welcomed Sarah warmly, noting with approval her well-fitting snuff brown tailored jacket and skirt that complimented her red-gold hair and a close fitting bonnet which framed her excited face, but raised an eyebrow at her severe hairstyle.

"I don't expect you to dress your hair so prissily; I hardly recognised you," softening this rebuke by offering her a cup of tea. "There is still time," with a nervous glance at the bracket clock on the wall.

Sarah nodded. "I have packed several pretty dresses that I had made for my trousseau," unaware that she had let slip something in her past that she wanted to keep hidden. Mrs. Merton was quick to note this, but it was not her place to probe.

She turned around as her son entered, a sturdy lad, with unnaturally plastered down hair, an endearing snub nose and a pair of mischievous grey eyes, that reminded her of Priscilla.

Harry eyed her cautiously, as his mother introduced him to add with a stern stare, "And I hope he will behave himself."

Sarah shook his hand, very conscious that she was being carefully assessed, before he stuck out his hand and politely murmured, "Pleased to meet you, Miss Danbury."

"Oh, for goodness sake, call me Sarah," she said in a friendly fashion. "From what I have gathered, the journey will be a long one, so I'm relying on you to show me the ropes, for I have never set foot out of Britain before, or sailed in a ship."

"Of course, it will be a pleasure, Sarah," returning the smile with a polite bow.

Sarah, who had failed to notice her employer's surprised relief, applauded her charge's good manners. They could not be faulted and took the opportunity to enquire what one did on board ship.

"Games, walking on deck and there's a children's playroom and usually the purser is a great gun. I'm hoping that one we get this time will be human," he remarked with deep feeling.

It was fortunate that she took these innocent words at their face value and it was just as well that she had been blessed with a sense of humour which her mother had never checked, knowing this trait would prove a Godsend, in smoothing the edges of life's little problems, but that sense of the ridiculous, was to be sorely tried on the voyage.

4

IT was a lovely sparkling afternoon when Mrs. Merton, Harry and Sarah set forth on their trip to the Far East, quickly finding themselves caught up in the hectic scene, as anxious passengers looked for seats on the boat-train, while their luggage was being swallowed up by the goods vans.

Mrs. Merton and Harry were already seated, Old Joe the coachman and another lad, in the next compartment, to see that the family's luggage was bestowed on the train and ship. No looking around frantically, for porters for Mrs. Merton, insisting that she travel with a modicum of fuss and discomfort.

Sarah had asked permission to watch out for her brother and was at the window, leaning far out, to scan the crowd, feeling very pleased with her appearance, that had attracted several smiles from gentlemen hurrying past.

Bertram had promised to come and see her off, if possible and there he was now just as the last bell sounded, his portly figure pushing his way through the throng of travellers, to grab her hand, Sarah thrilled, presenting a smiling face, mirroring her happiness.

He greeted Mrs. Merton and Harry and there was just enough time for him to wish them all *bon voyage*, before the train began to move, thrusting the posy of flowers that he had brought her, into her hands.

The family returned to their seats, Sarah sitting down with a sigh. "He remembered," she said simply, as they made themselves comfortable.

Sarah sat staring out of the window at the flying countryside, but seeing nothing, only now realising fully, that she was about to leave her homeland, knowing a moment of panic, her thoughts on the Stranger. With a blinding clarity of mind, she knew that she had loved him for weeks now, but had never allowed herself to acknowledge it. There had always been at the back of her mind, that the whole scenario had only been a hoax played by a friend of Edward's. He had known that she was Edward's fianced bride and was probably even now, making marriage arrangements of his own and hope died, berating herself for being a peagoose, her face draining of all colour.

Mrs. Merton had cast her several anxious glances, aware that there must have been some tragedy in her past. Had there been a broken engagement, for she had mentioned a trousseau.

Sarah catching her employer's worried frown, smiled as the lady said bracingly, "A long sea trip will dispel any cobwebs you may have, my dear."

The train steamed into Southampton docks and disgorged its passengers and there lay the liner towering above them, Sarah's eyes wide, gaping at the huge bulk, keeping close to Mrs. Merton's side, with an urge to hang on to her skirts, afraid that in this milling crowd, she would be swept away. Passengers lined the rails, while others were still embarking. All was hustle and bustle, trunks littering every space, or so it seemed, as porters shouted and people looked harassed. Then there were those who were there to bid farewell to friends and relatives, whom they might never see again.

Sarah now knew how wise Mrs. Merton had been to bring her sister's coachman and the other lad, who carried their trunks and other luggage up the gangplank and into their cabins, whether it was allowed or not.

"This is why I always arrive early, Sarah. As you can see all is bedlam and if one arrived late, it is even more so," taking the pins out of her hat.

"I wouldn't have thought all this activity could be any worse," she replied, looking around the small, well furnished cabin, with interest.

Sarah helped her employer to unpack then rang the bell for the stewardess to have her trunk taken down to the hold and to give orders for morning tea. The stewardess, introducing herself as Ethel, was a friendly, kindly soul, very willing to help in any way she could, saying aside to Sarah, that that dear lady was going to be a bad traveller.

"Mark my words, Miss! Know them immediate, m'darling. Now you'll be no problem at all!" and went off, white skirts swishing.

Sarah slipped away to her cabin, which she was to share with Harry. Where was Harry? In all the mêlée she had forgotten him and rushed back to Mrs. Merton's cabin, to be calmed of her fears.

"Don't worry, dear, he's probably gone to see if there are any other boys he can fraternize with; he'll be back. Now let's go and say farewell to the land of our birth."

As they stood at the rail, Harry joined them, giving Sarah a huge grin,

158

saying that he had met several boys of his own age. Passengers were still coming aboard, but their numbers had decreased to a trickle, Mrs. Merton a little upset at the sadness of some of the farewells.

"Just look at that couple over there," nodding towards a girl and a man locked in each other's arms. "There are no more words to be said, poor dears and it takes such an age for the ship to finally leave. So very distressing for all concerned! Nothing is more traumatic than to say goodbye. That is why I ask my relations and friends, not to come and see me off," wiping away a tear, surreptitiously.

"I'm going back to a dear husband, but a lot of these people won't see their loved ones again, for a long time."

The final 'all ashore' warning was sounded and the gang plank heaved up, the ship slowly moving away from the wharf, the visitors becoming smaller and smaller, most of them openly weeping.

Mrs. Merton turned away, with the prosaic suggestion that they all go and have tea. "Come along, young man," noticing her son edging away, much to Harry's chagrin.

She led the way into one of the lounges, where tea and cakes were being served, the passengers slowly filling up the tables.

Sarah still mesmerized, by what was going on around her, heard only half of the conversation her employer was having with an acquaintance, until she said, "Oh good, I also prefer the second sitting. Will see you then?" turning back to Sarah as the lady went in search of a table. "I always find someone who I've met previously," she said gloomily. "There are some I could do without. Now let's go and find the purser and become acquainted with him. He's the man who listens to all our woes."

Peter Fenn was a man in his late thirties, pleasant with a conciliatory manner. "Well, that is what he is paid for," when Sarah remarked that he would be a help if she ever found herself at a standstill, immediately thinking of Harry, who later on, obligingly offered to show her the ship; the decks they could use, the children's sections and where the bathrooms and water closets were, the passenger lounges, all sumptuously and beautifully furnished, the dining-rooms no less so, with pristine napery, shining cutlery and glassware, Sarah not quite believing that all this was to be her home for many weeks on end.

"We're lucky, Sarah," he said, as they retraced their steps, "that Father, when he booked our return journey, was able to get us cabins with portholes. Not every cabin has one, you know. When we came over, me and Dirk, my brother," he explained, seeing the query in her raised eyebrow, "our cabin had no porthole. It was really horrible, dreadfully hot and stuffy. We took our pillows and slept on deck. Mother never knew.

She would only have worried," he added simply.

They returned to Mrs. Merton, Harry politely drawing out a chair for her and then to ask his mother's permission, if he could go and explore further, she admonishing him not to get into any mischief.

Harry hurried away, thankful that from now on, no child would be allowed in the adult lounges.

Sarah began talking about all that she had seen. "Mrs. Merton you have a very good son. Now I feel that I, perhaps, won't get so lost."

She looked doubtful, but refrained from any comment, as a large lady bore down on them, saying gushingly,

"Why, dear Daphne! This is a lovely surprise. May I join you ladies?" her glance going to Sarah, inquisitively.

Sarah was introduced to Mrs. Faulkner, surprised when her employer added, "This is a daughter of a dear friend of mine in England. I thought it an excellent chance to give the child an opportunity to see something of the world, before she settles down."

Sarah, taken aback by this tarradiddle, did not respond, except to choke down laughter and return the lady's greeting.

Evidently, her employer did not want this acquaintance, to think she was incapable of looking after herself or Harry.

"A splendid idea, Daphne," she gushed, "and dear Miss Danbury, I'm sure you'll enjoy the voyage, prodigiously," to continue, stroking her long, well-manicured fingers. "Daphne, both our children are now attending Harrow. You know my husband was educated there, I think and we could not but follow suit, with our sons. Sons are so much easier to launch, than girls, don't you agree, but where is Harry? I presume you must have brought him over with Dirk? He's to go to Eton?"

Mrs. Merton could only nod, but did, eventually, manage to get a word in. "I suppose you are getting off at Singapore, Winnie? Heard of Cliff's promotion. Congratulations, or is it commiserations?"

"Thank you," with a heavy sigh. "Cliff is to take up a position there, but I hate all these upheavals and hope that our furniture has already arrived, before I get there," a worried frown creasing her brow.

When that lady finally excused herself, Mrs. Merton turned to Sarah, meeting her dancing eyes. "My dear, from now on please call me Aunt Daphne. It will be so much easier," with a gurgle of mirth.

"That was kind of you, Mrs. — Aunt Daphne."

"Not at all, it will be more comfortable for you. I would not have you ostracized for the world! And what is more, it will make life simpler when we reach Hong Kong, for the English community are high sticklers, even more so than London society. Out there we're more British than the British at home, but I can't blame people. I'm that way myself and why not? Standards must not drop when one lives in a British colony," twinkling at Sarah. "And who knows, you just might meet a handsome gentleman here on board ship, or even in Hong Kong?" looking arch, Sarah's smile a little forced.

The next passenger to avail herself of the empty chair, was a slight, pretty, fair-haired girl, with large pansy-brown eyes, who asked shyly if they minded her joining them, saying her name was Agnes Picton and was going out to Hong Kong to marry Dick Forbes and that she was all alone, all this said in a quiet, uncertain voice, as she seated herself.

Mrs. Merton sat up, showing sudden interest. "I know Dick Forbes, but was not aware that he was even courting a girl back home. Was this very sudden?" she asked inquisitively.

Agnes shook her curls, animation lending character to her face. "I've known Dick forever. His parents live next door and when he was on his last leave, we became very friendly and he promised to write," a demure dimple peeping from her cheek and a warm glow stealing into her pale face at the memory, "But I was very surprised and happy, when he wrote and asked me to marry him.

"He also wrote to Papa, who was delighted," showing them her engagement ring. "There are a lot of us at home," she explained shyly. "Dick even sent over my ticket and spending money," with awe.

A comfortable silence fell as she drank her tea, that Mrs. Merton had ordered for her.

Agnes went on to enquire what Hong Kong was really like as Dick had been vague about conditions out there.

Mrs. Merton explained. "My family and I are very happy there and it's a pleasant place in which to live, the summers though are trying, being very hot and humid, but one gets acclimatized. There is quite a large English community and lots of Chinese, of course," smiling kindly, but this did not appear to comfort Agnes, who had become a little tearful.

"If — if I'd known of this huge ship and the weeks and weeks it will take," gulping, "perhaps I wouldn't have accepted Dick's offer," her sensitive mouth quivering. "And I — I don't know anyone," dabbing her eyes, as a child would have done.

Sarah placed a comforting arm about her shoulders. "You'll soon make friends," she promised, who had a great deal of sympathy for this girl, forgetting that she was probably, about the same age and was pleased when Agnes cheered up. "And I'm sure Aunt Daphne here, will chaperone you, if you so wish," but there was no response from this lady. Was Aunt Daphne already beginning to feel squeamish, Sarah wondered, with concern.

★ ★ ★

Later that night Sarah sank gratefully into her bunk. It had been a full day, Harry already asleep on the top one. He had very politely given her the choice and was pleased when she suggested that as he was the younger, he had better take the top one, her rating going up a notch or two.

She had had a leisurely salt water bath, with a small bowl of fresh water in which to rinse her face. Mrs. Merton had not gone down to dinner, asking that she might have a light meal sent to her in bed.

"I must warn you, dear, that I'm a shockingly bad traveller," she had confessed, looking extremely washed out. "I do hope you'll be all right, because Harry does need someone to keep an eye on him. I become prostrate for days," a shudder shaking her at the very thought.

Sarah had assured her that she was feeling well, which seemed to calm her. The stewardess had arrived, which enabled Sarah to go in to dinner and afterwards go up on deck for awhile, finding a sheltered nook to breathe in the fresh, salty air, not quite believing that she was where she was, or the turn her life had taken. Her thoughts, once again, turning to the Stranger, wondering if she had dreamt the whole affair.

Suddenly she was conscious of someone coming up the companionway and slipped into the shadows, not wanting to meet anyone.

On her way back to her cabin, she had peeped in to see how Aunt Daphne fared to find her sleeping peacefully. Now she closed her eyes, praying that she might not succumb to seasickness. What would she do? There was Harry — but sleep took her. It had been a tiring day.

She slept well that night and the brandy and hot milk the stewardess had suggested for both ladies, acted as a splendid soporific.

The following morning Sarah unaffected by the pitching and rolling of the ship, which she later described in a letter to Bertram 'like a drunk man', went to see how Mrs. Merton was to find that she had been extremely ill most of the night and was now so exhausted that she could barely speak, but did manage to ask Sarah again, to keep an eye on Harry.

"This happens every trip," explained Ethel, "certain folk just go down like ninepins, their poor insides churning around," she said with ghoulish sympathy. "You don't look as if you're been affected, Miss?" Sarah shaking her head, feeling helpless.

Ethel had turned again to her patient. "Dear Mrs. Merton, please eat this piece of bread and butter," she pleaded, "it's an empty stomach you have and you'll feel much better when we're out of these rough waters," but all her patient could do was groan and turn away.

"Ethel," said Sarah quickly, "I must go and see what Harry is doing, please excuse me," to make a hurried exit.

Harry wasn't at all pleased to see Sarah walk into the dining-room, where all the children were being served breakfast, uttering a gruff "good morning" saying he was too old to be treated like a baby, frowning darkly.

She glanced around at all the parents, sitting with their offspring, raising an enquiring brow "I won't put you to the blush, Harry," she said quietly. "I'm also going to have breakfast now. My stomach feels as if it has a huge hole in it. I couldn't possibly wait until 9 o'clock. What would you advise me to have," with a glance at the menu.

He was immediately mollified, introducing her to the children and their parents at their table, suggesting scrambled eggs with fish on toast. "The eggs are still fresh," and went on to suggest several other dishes, to add with admiration, "You're a great gun, Sarah. A lot of people are really ill. I looked in on Mother and she's as sick as a horse, always is for the first few days."

"I also visited her. Ethel is with her, I'll go back after I have finished my breakfast. I'm already feeling better at the sight of this food," thanking the waiter. "How did you manage when you came over. Oh, I forgot, your brother was with you."

"Dirk's all right. Mother didn't once come to the table with us," reverting to his original grouse, but that did not stop him from ladling fruit compote into his mouth as if he had a train to catch.

"Harry! Oh, I've had the most ghastly thought. I don't know how to treat a painful stomach."

"Don't suffer from them," his mouth still full.

"Perhaps, but you will if you eat so quickly. Haven't you yet learned about the digestive system?" spreading butter on her toast, with a concerned frown at her charge.

"Of course, but I don't pay much attention to stuff like that, so you need not be worried about me," he ended up kindly and ordered a second helping.

The high seas abated and Sarah managed to persuade Mrs. Merton to get dressed and go on deck, where they found a shady corner, glad for the brisk breeze, for the weather had warmed up considerably. She also managed to get her employer, still weak and empty to drink a cup of tea and nibble a sweet biscuit, when a waiter came around, trundling a trolley, laden with dainty china and plates of good things to eat, this a service for people too lazy to go to the lounge. The lunch bell rang and Mrs. Merton was able to walk to the dining-room, managing to eat a fair meal, much to Sarah's relief.

Sarah found her days busy, trying hard not to be too obviously watching her charge, to find keeping tabs on Harry was no sinecure, his small, wiry body never still and no wonder Aunt Daphne needed someone to keep an eye on him. Fortunately, he had made friends with other choice spirits and at meal times was so hungry that he did not object to her presence.

Aunt Daphne, though, did insist that her son be in bed before the second sitting of dinner, Ethel to peep in every now and again. Fortunately, tiredness sent him to sleep quickly, Sarah feeling at liberty to enjoy quiet dinners with Aunt Daphne and to join in the festivities of the evening, Sarah finding that Aunt Daphne was a person who liked to stay up late and was thoroughly, enjoying life on an ocean liner. The lachrymose lady who had interviewed her, had quite disappeared, Sarah careful that Harry's pranks, and they were numerous, did not reach her ears. That was what she was paid for, after all.

Harry and the other boys, naturally did not relish the idea of being cooped up in the supervised play area, but his mother insisted that he be there for, at least, two hours after morning tea.

"Sarah is entitled to that time off, Harry," with a level look at her son, who nodded grudgingly. This enabled Sarah to take part and enjoy the deck activities.

As the days passed, Aunt Daphne

and Sarah, became increasingly uneasy and concerned about Agnes and a certain young man, who was paying her marked attention. They were dancing now, he holding her far too close, every now and again kissing her hand, that he was holding against his chest, Aunt Daphne's eyebrows raising.

"They do appear to be much struck with each other," agreed Sarah.

"Oh, poor Dick!" murmured Aunt Daphne, "and I was so hoping that Agnes would have a level head, for Dick can be terribly scatterbrained at times. Tch!" shaking her head, disapprovingly.

"I hope she has told him she's engaged. I see she's still wearing her ring, which was wise of her."

"Perhaps, but that is not stopping young Anthony Timms from flirting with her. Oh dear! but I've found that people on board ship tend to throw away all values and be far more forward than they would dare to be in normal society."

"Is there anything you can do, Aunt Daphne?"

She shook her head. "Agnes would not thank us and could make matters worse. Let's hope she comes to her senses."

The two ladies turned their attention back to the excellent, four-piece orchestra that was playing a Viennese waltz, when a young man approached their table, Sarah's foot tapping to the music, introducing himself as Jason Goodall and asked Aunt Daphne's permission to dance with Sarah, who gave her gracious consent, with a pleased smile, watching them as they walked on to the dance floor. A very presentable young man, good looking with fair hair, his face, attractively, sun tanned.

"I've noticed you several times, Miss Danbury," he smiled, as he whirled her round, "but each time you appear to have lost something, I'm intrigued!"

"Not something, someone," she retorted with deep feeling. "I'm helping Mrs. Merton, who has been ill, to look after her son. Harry is an very inventive, nine year old youngster."

"My sympathies," chuckling. "And where are you destined for, may I ask?" as they danced to the ever changing dip of the ship, finding it exhilarating.

"Hong Kong," and went on in her friendly fashion, "I'm the daughter of a friend of Mrs. Merton's," parroting her employer's tarradiddle, "and she very kindly asked me to accompany her."

"To look after her son, I presume?"

She nodded, with a grin that lit up her mischievous eyes.

"Well, you'll certainly be able to say that you had regular exercise on the trip."

"And you, Sir, where are you destined for?" the deck tilting again, forcing them to race down it's length. "I'm really enjoying this," she gasped, falling into delighted, shared laughter.

"My destination, for the time being, is Singapore, where I work for Forsythe's, a London based firm, textiles, imports, exports, that kind of thing, so all my travelling is in the line of duty, as we have dealings with most of the Eastern countries. This time I was sent to London to report to the parent company on the fierce competition we're experiencing from the House of Mac Gowan, based in Hong Kong. Perhaps you'll even meet Simon Mac Gowan, a very clever, cunning man."

The dance ended and he took her back to Mrs. Merton, who handed her her fan, her gaze affectionate. It certainly was a very hot night.

"My dear, I'm so glad to see you enjoying yourself. Mr. Goodall appears to be a most pleasant young man, but I should think a philanderer?"

Sarah chuckled. "Well, he does travel for his firm — "

"Ah, just as bad as any travelling salesman?" she hinted darkly.

"Aunt Daphne, I do believe you're warning me off. He said something about being in competition with a very astute gentleman in Hong Kong, so perhaps he's a very superior salesman? Evidently both their firms deal in the same commodities," she murmured with amusement.

"I do hope you make friends, dear, but these kind of affairs, never last," came the crisp retort.

From then on Sarah in her free time, was plunged into all the activities that the ship could offer, Jason being her partner; in the deck games and dancing with her, under star studded skies, Sarah loving every minute of it, this exhilaration being strange to her.

The ship arrived at Gibraltar and it was with regret that Sarah could not go ashore, where carriages were waiting to take passengers sightseeing, amid a lot of laughter, but reminded herself firmly, that her first duty was to Aunt Daphne and Harry and it would have been unwise and unladylike to go ashore without a male escort, Aunt Daphne having visited the Rock before. Jason had said that he was sorry that he could not take her, but had to call on his company's agent.

That evening, all the passengers were able to enjoy the Mediterranean fruits that had been brought aboard and dinner was a merry meal, some guest bringing up the legend that if the apes on the Rock were to disappear or die out, then the British would no longer hold Gibraltar. A hot debate followed that overflowed to other tables.

Sarah had written to her family and to the Countess, long newsy letters which she had posted in the ship's postbox, expecting none in return, as she would be going back on this ship.

The purser, Peter Fenn, also had been very attentive and they became firm friends, as she had had to call on him on several occasions, when she had not been able to find Harry. He was a man in his mid thirties already going bald and had been most diplomatic, vanishing before Harry could catch sight of him.

Aunt Daphne was thrilled and though she did not approve of shipboard romances, at least the child was enjoying herself, but there was still a sadness about her when her face was in repose. It must be ghastly to have to earn one's living, even though that work was to be nursing, a commendable choice, but extremely exhaustive work, shuddering at the very thought.

The next port of call was Malta, Aunt Daphne saying that as she had seen all these places, would much rather sit under an awning, as it was too hot for any unusual exercise, to add, "You'll be able to visit these cities on your return journey, dear," she consoled. "By the time we arrive in Hong Kong, the summer heat and humidity should have abated a little. I quickly learnt to discard several of my nether garments and you'll do the same. They're totally unnecessary. Mind you, I know some elderly ladies, bless them, heartily disapprove and suffer severe skin problems in consequence, as you can imagine."

Sarah had already done so, but saw

no reason for her to say so.

She leant on the rail watching the people below as they settled themselves into small boats, with gaily coloured awnings, after much gesticulating from the boat owners. From where she stood, she could see that the city had very steep streets, some only steps, the buildings dazzling white in the morning sunshine, also many fortifications and cannon emplacements.

Sarah turned, her attention caught by a ship in full sail, leaving the harbour. "Oh, what a beautiful sight," she breathed.

"It is a lovely sight," agreed Aunt Daphne. "It is probably, carrying either opium or tea."

"Opium?" gasped Sarah, turning around abruptly.

"Which I abhor," her voice filled with disgust. "The victims of this habit are legion," wrinkling her shapely nose fastidiously, refusing to say more.

Silenced, Sarah glanced around, wondering what had happened to

Harry, he had been with them a few moments ago. She excused herself quickly, wondering what mischief he was up to, but for a change, found him in the children's library, his nose in a book and retraced her steps. Had he looked too innocent?

That night Sarah crawled into her bunk, not knowing whether she should have a fit of the vapours or a hearty laugh. Peter Fenn, the purser, usually managed to maintain some discipline amongst the boys, but this escapade of Harry's had escaped his notice, unfortunately. He had other duties to perform, as people disembarked while others went sightseeing. And there lay the culprit, sleeping as peacefully as any angel.

As the voyage had progressed, the children arrived at a stage when all activities became boring, this was particularly prevalent amongst the boys. She supposed an outburst of naughtiness had to be expected. It was just unfortunate though, that Harry had chosen the Captain's cat. Finding a shady nook, he had set to, with the aid of her curved nail scissors, to cut away the Captain's initials on the animal's flank. The cat was a short haired one, so the markings were most prominent.

Captain Hadding had been furious, but that evening at dinner, he made reference to it, with a jovial chuckle, saying that this prank would certainly be written in the log book. The passengers had thought it hilarious and Harry, when asked how he had managed to keep the animal still, said that it just lay there, purring.

Aunt Daphne's eyebrows flew up, glancing wildly at Sarah, who immediately felt it was all her fault.

Unfortunately the evidence of this prank would last a long time. Nobody was going to forget it.

Harry was called into his parent's cabin and returned later to Sarah, not a little subdued.

"Mother's not very pleased with me,

I'm afraid," he confessed, "but she did tell me what the Captain had said," brightening up.

"A very forgiving man," she said sternly, trying to still a quivering lip.

"I thought it a great lark and what is more Sarah, I found out that the Captain keeps a pair of tongs to curl his moustache," he said with marked satisfaction.

"Oh, no! You — you haven't — ?" her voice not her own.

"No, I haven't been in his quarters," he retorted hotly. "Some other chap told me," but chuckled at her sigh of relief.

★ ★ ★

The food on the ship was excellent, Sarah especially appreciative, enjoying it to the full, plus the fact that she had not helped cook it. As she glanced around the dining-room filled with chattering people, she murmured, "Everyone of us destined for somewhere else, but now linked together for just a little while."

"Are you usually so fanciful, dear?" smiled Aunt Daphne, helping herself to another plate of fresh fruit salad, knowing it would not add inches to her waistline.

At each of their stops, the ship had taken on fresh fruit, vegetables and poultry.

"No, I always thought of myself as being a very prosaic person," Sarah surprised at herself. "Aunt Daphne, I'm so very grateful to you for bringing me on this trip," with a break in her voice.

"And I think you should have a James' Powder tonight, my girl. What would I do without you? It is I who is beholden to you. I consider myself extremely fortunate that you were sent to me," with deep sincerity, to change the subject, "We will be stopping at Alexandria tomorrow, where the passengers will be able to visit the Pyramids and the Sphinx and then on to Suez, where we sail, in convoy, through several lakes. Thank goodness, this Canal has been built, otherwise we would have had to endure the rigours of having to go around the Cape of Good Hope and that trip took forever. Thanks be also, for steamships," shuddering dramatically.

"This service has also enabled us to have more regular mail between Hong Kong and Britain. So comforting, dear, to hear from loved ones more often," smiling at Sarah's intent expression.

This young companion of hers had blossomed, her tawny hair now having a healthy glow to it and she had even put on a little weight, which suited her. Also her features, though unassuming, were more often lit by her happy smile and merry green eyes, that twinkled quite delightfully. A far more contented person, thought Mrs. Merton happily.

"Sarah, I feel that I know you much better now and won't go all prim on me when I ask you why you had to take this post? You're a gently reared

187

girl from a good family, so why?"

"Of course I won't mind, Aunt Daphne, it's very simple, really. My sister-in-law and I don't see eye-to-eye. Louise resents my presence in her home," with a rueful smile. "I had reached the point when I could no longer tolerate the situation. I think Priscilla, my niece mentioned this?"

"Ah, yes! I suppose your relation has a daughter who is not as beautiful as you are?"

"Aunt Daphne, I've never considered myself beautiful," she protested.

"Nonsense, my dear!"

The following day was overcast, humid and uncomfortable, without even a breeze to freshen the atmosphere, but by late afternoon, it cleared, the sunset beyond description, fiery red, orange and blue streamers shooting from the edges of the earth.

Jason found Sarah at the rail, utterly absorbed by this magnificence. They had become firm friends, enjoying the deck games when she was free and the dancing, Sarah coming in for a great deal of teasing from Aunt Daphne. He was very well read and Sarah could not deny that she enjoyed his company, acknowledging to Aunt Daphne that he was an extraordinarily easy person to talk to, even their silences were easy.

"It is indescribably beautiful," she whispered as he placed a hand over hers, a companionable silence falling, as they watched the colours fading and then to stroll along the deck, a lovely, happy interlude, with never a thought to what her charge was doing, his mother supervising his supper.

They stopped by mutual consent, Jason turning her to him. "Sarah, what about coming ashore with me at Singapore and then take the boat when it calls in at the port on its return journey. Surely Mrs. Merton can look after young Harry for the rest of the trip?"

"And what would I do there?" came her amused query.

"Marry me, of course," he replied

audaciously, with a grin, amused at her look of utter astonishment.

"Me?" the word coming out as a squeak.

"Yes you, Miss Sarah Danbury and why the surprise? We've enjoyed each other's company tremendously, no gainsaying that," his hazel eyes suddenly tender.

"I'm very honoured, Jason, but all this — " waving a hand vaguely.

"Is too unreal; you don't trust that sunset, because it has disappeared? I can understand that, plus the fact that this life on board is too superficial, for anyone to be sure of any friendship?"

She nodded, not willing to take him seriously. "I am aware that romances flourish on board ship, but this feeling you have for me, can't be real?"

"It is for me," he insisted gently. "Disembark with me at Singapore and we'll get to know each other better and you can stay with the Bishop and his wife."

"No, Jason," her reply kindly,

accompanied by a chuckle. "I promised to look after Harry for the whole trip. Poor Aunt Daphne is a bad traveller and even now does not feel really well and I don't know what Mother would say," lowering her eyes to conceal their gleam, remembering again, the fib of her employer's.

Jason heaved an exaggerated sigh, accepting defeat. "Oh well. Can't win 'em all," submitting with good grace.

Sarah smiled at him. "Mr. Goodall you know, more than I, that this kind of sea magic, never lasts. Now be truthful."

"Perhaps, but I'm determined I shall meet this ship when she returns," he promised seriously.

"I can't honestly say that I really know if I will be returning on this boat. My aunt has not been specific, I've just presumed."

"Don't worry, I'll scan the passenger lists. I want to see you again, Sarah, to show you around Singapore, for you to see what kind of life we live.

There is nothing superficial about that country."

He turned her around, tightening his grip on her fingers and led her to where Aunt Daphne was once more reclining.

The following morning they again met, Sarah taking the initiative, forestalling any chance of unease between them. "What would you have done if I'd accepted your proposal?" she demanded. "I might have been desperate for a husband," her eyes laughing up at him.

He bowed, with hand on heart. "I would have been delighted," he replied gallantly, his eyes soulful.

"I think you're just a flirt, Mr. Jason Goodall," she replied indignantly.

"But I will meet you again on your return journey," was his serious reply, his eyes very steady.

She nodded, turning away, leaving him looking after her, with a serious expression. Perhaps it was better this way, a chuckle escaping him, but what an unusual girl and one that he would not forget in a hurry.

As Sarah got into her bed later that night, she wondered if she should have thought more about Jason's offer, but the Stranger was once more behind her eyelids, realizing that it had been some time since she had thought about him. He was only a phantom now. Had she dreamt the whole episode, born of her need to be loved and the fear of an arranged marriage? Even his face had become blurred and unreal. Her cheeks were wet as she dropped off to sleep.

The following morning, as Sarah dressed, wondered if the meeting with Jason would be a little awkward, but it wasn't. They were back on their old friendly footing, as the voyage progressed.

They had called in at Bombay and now, tomorrow, they would awake to find themselves docked in Singapore's harbour, both Aunt Daphne and Sarah thankful that the trip was nearly over.

A dinner dance had been especially

arranged by the entertainment committee, as a number of passengers would be leaving the ship. It was a gala evening, Sarah thankful, that she had one of her trousseau gowns to fall back on, Aunt Daphne approving the sea-green voile, the material light and cool, the tiny puffed sleeves holding up the low-cut, tight bodice, the skirt in flounces down to her tiny satin shod feet, her hair simply tied back with a big bow, several strands being allowed to fall on either side of her face. Harry's comment was that she was 'bang up to the nines' and when he was old enough he would ask her to dance. Coming from her charge, Sarah thought this high praise indeed.

The evening was a great success, Aunt Daphne making no demur when Jason claimed Sarah for most of the dances. It would do her companion no harm to try her wings and was a sensible young woman, one she had become very much attached to. Nobody else even raised an eyebrow, but she was not so sanguine as her glance sought out Agnes and Anthony Timms, the young lady very tearful and downcast, no doubt because the gentleman would be leaving the following morning.

The time of disembarking was all hustle and bustle, as passengers said goodbye, Jason giving Aunt Daphne and Sarah great hugs, thanking them for making the trip so enjoyable and memorable, with a glance in Sarah's direction, before striding off down the gangway, the ladies waving from the rail. He gave them a final salute before disappearing into the customs' building.

Suddenly Aunt Daphne grabbed Sarah's arm and said in a horrified voice, pointing as she did so, "It's Agnes Picton, going down with young Timms and she has hand luggage. Oh dear!" visibly shaken.

"Perhaps he has promised to take her sightseeing and perhaps, that's his luggage," replied Sarah charitably. "Nothing wrong in that, surely?"

"You wouldn't have gone off with

Jason, would you? Her silly act is quite reprehensible! And what about poor Dick, she is his fiance, after all. We know him well, a quiet, shy young man, who works in my husband's office. Now I feel responsible for not looking after her properly," she wailed, beating the rail with her fists.

Sarah threw a comforting arm around her, trying to comfort her distress. "You haven't been really well, this whole trip and have dozed a lot of the time," excusing her, but this did not mend matters.

"That's no excuse. I feel dreadful!" close to tears.

"Aunt Daphne, let's wait until this afternoon. We'll then see if Agnes comes back. We sail at five," she reminded her, soothingly.

"Hm! The attentions he has been giving her over the weeks, makes me wonder," she added darkly.

They turned away from the rails, Aunt Daphne and Sarah to seek their deck chairs, Harry hurrying off to find out how many of his friends were still aboard.

Sarah looked around her at the clean, scrubbed deck, a gentle breeze stirring the striped awnings. "I suppose I must go and see where Harry is," she said lazily, but Aunt Daphne laid a detaining hand on her arm.

"You are off duty, dear. He can look after himself," she murmured comfortably at the edge of sleep.

It was at dinner that night, in a depleted dining room, when Aunt Daphne after glancing around the room, said in 'I told you so' voice that Agnes was not at her table and appeared to crumple in her chair. "Oh, poor Dick! What are his feelings going to be when he learns that she is not on the boat? Oh, dear!" very much put out, a subdued Sarah enquiring,

"Do you know if this happens often?" as she helped herself to fresh salads, the waiter was holding out to her.

"Yes, it does I'm afraid. Young men sent out to the colonies, leave behind

197

sweethearts and over the months, perhaps years of exchanging letters, the man asks the girl to come out and now you know what could happen. Not always though. So sad!"

"Please tell me a little about Hong Kong," trying to break the gloomy thoughts that had taken hold of them both. "My brother told me that the Queen was not amused at the annexation."

Aunt Daphne nodded. "If I remember correctly, her Majesty and other high officials in the government pooh-poohed it as a worthless rock, for you must know, that Hong Kong is extremely mountainous. Literally everything has to be brought in, down to the most basic of requirements, as the country has very little flat land. The Chinese do manage to grow rice and vegetables for their own use on small plots of flat ground. They also keep animals for milk and meat. Other than that there is very little arable land available.

"What her Majesty and her ministers failed to take into account though, was the enormous potential for trade between Britain and the Far East, plus the fact that it had the safest deep water harbour in the area, where ships could be careened and overhauled. Not forgetting that we are subjected to typhoons, so our harbour is a Godsend for all ships. And when you see your first Junk, you'll know you're in the Far East. Come dear, let's retire to the lounge and I'll continue with your education," laying down her napkin with a chuckle, Sarah pleased to see that Aunt Daphne had regained some of her equilibrium.

As soon as they were seated, Sarah naturally, wanted to know what Junks were, accepting the coffee being handed to her.

"They're Chinese boats, painted dark brown with fluted brown sails, the rigging completely different from the usual sailing vessels. Most attractive, different!"

"And the houses?" Sarah wanted to know.

"Well, you'll never see one with a pitched roof. A few years back we suffered a devastating typhoon, that ripped flimsy dwellings, sucking up everything in its path, even people," and shuddered as she recalled how they had had to stay in their underground cellars for thirty-six hours. "Hong Kong is an island to which, in 1860, the peninsula of Kowloon was added. And now, dear, I really must have my after dinner nap," and promptly did just that, much to Sarah's amusement, but opened one eye to say, "Chinese delicacies are snakes, lizards, rice and noodles," which left Sarah thankful that she had had her dinner.

It was the last day of the trip, some passengers jubilant that they would be restored to their loved ones, Mrs. Merton amongst them, others apprehensive of what Hong Kong would hold for them.

That afternoon Aunt Daphne and

Sarah were sitting in their favourite place under an awning, Harry completely wrapped up doing a jigsaw puzzle on a tray, that he had somehow, purloined from the kitchens, looking as if butter wouldn't melt in his mouth, his mother gazing down at him fondly.

"I miss Jason," murmured Sarah lazily. "I liked him immensely," remembering the fun they had enjoyed. Would he meet the boat on her return journey, she wondered and what would her reaction be? She shook her head, she did not know.

"A very charming young man," agreed Aunt Daphne, surprisingly awake, returning to her book. It had to be handed in that evening. Silence followed for some time, until she closed the book and rose to her feet. "I'm going to start packing dear, and advise you do the same. Tomorrow will be chaotic. Come along, young man."

Sarah was helping Aunt Daphne to pack, her trunk all ready and standing open, the last item of clothing laying neatly on the top, needing only the last minute items to be packed, when suddenly there was a commotion outside their cabin.

"I suppose wrong trunks have been delivered to wrong cabins," said Aunt Daphne, resignedly. "It does happen," but Sarah decided to investigate and was met by several irate ladies, one whispering to Sarah that every lavatory door on their deck had been locked.

"But — but who could have done that?" she queried, utterly taken aback. "And how?"

"My dear, it's quite easy. There's that space under the doors. Disgraceful!" she muttered angrily.

Sarah nodded. "A child could get under there, easily," she agreed, with a sinking feeling in the pit of her stomach and hurriedly excused herself, to begin searching for Harry, trying not to let nervous giggles escape her. She found her charge, with several other boys, in the Purser's office, plus parents.

"Ah, Sarah," murmured a harassed

Peter Fenn. "I presume you have heard what has happened?" Sarah nodding mutely. "Unfortunately, this has reached the Captain's ears. Heads will no doubt roll," wiping his perspiring face. "I'm afraid I have to take you all to see the Captain," looking around the assembled company, who were unnervingly quiet.

The youths were lined up on the left of the Captain, as he sat at his desk, parents and Sarah on his other side, Harry careful not to meet Sarah's accusing eyes.

Captain Hadding was stroking his moustache and Sarah could have sworn it was to hide a smile. "Parents, a very serious charge has been laid against your sons, that of causing grave discomfort to the passengers and staff of this ship," to end dramatically. "I have a grave suspicion that this boat of mine is bound to be the laughing stock of the whole of the P & O Line and in every club in Hong Kong and perhaps even in the Mother Country."

"A bit of an exaggeration, wouldn't you say?" commented a male voice at Sarah's side.

She nodded, deeply concerned that this was all her fault that Harry was numbered amongst these culprits, ashamed that she had failed in her duty. What was Aunt Daphne going to say? Most parents, she noticed, were also concerned.

The Captain continued. "Parents, I want you to suggest the most effective punishment to fit the crime. Throw them into the hold?" his brows beetling over the now sheepish boys.

A father raised his hand. "Sir, I would first like to apologize, on behalf of all of us and suggest our sons go now and unlock every door in both ladies' and gents' lavatories'. There the lads will have to face the wrath of both sexes and good luck to them."

There was only one who dissented, a tightly laced matron, making her rather like a pouter-pigeon, whom the Captain waved aside.

"What an excellent suggestion," he applauded, with ghoulish relish, the boys aghast and were more so when the Captain added that he wanted to see them, without their parents, when the job was done, but did add a palliative that only the ladies' privy doors were to be opened, leaving the lads completely deflated, as they filed out of the cabin. Several parents and Sarah stayed behind to apologize again, for the boys' bad behaviour, the Captain now his jovial self again, turned to Sarah to say with a chuckle, "Please convey to Harry's mother that I would deem it a favour if, when she next travels, to please leave Harry at home. My poor cat is marked for life, I fear."

Sarah returned to the cabins, but Aunt Daphne was not there, to find her on deck enjoying the last rays of the sun throwing pink fingers up into the blue heaven, thankful that the journey was soon to end.

Sarah sat down beside her soberly.

"Aunt Daphne I've failed you," and went on to tell her about the locked doors. "I should have minded Harry with more care," she confessed.

"Was that what all the fuss was about?" was all her employer could find to say. "Oh dear!" her only comment becoming a little flurried but, seeing Sarah's distress said kindly, "It wasn't your fault, dear, you were helping me to pack, remember? I must admit though, that this prank goes beyond the pale. The Captain must have been very annoyed and rightly so. What has he done about the culprits?" she enquired, a little apprehensively.

"Captain Hadding asked for some ideas from the parents on what punishment should be applied," and went on to tell her what had been suggested.

Aunt Daphne was aghast. "A very good idea, I suppose," a little weakly, "but in the Ladies'?"

At that moment the Purser appeared, Mrs. Merton offering her sincere apologies, on behalf of her son.

He grinned. "This was a new one on me, Ma'am," he admitted ruefully. "In all the years I've been in this Line, no boy has ever thought of this one, thank goodness!" adding with deep feeling. "Mrs. Merton, your son and the rest of the lads, will only be available again, at the Children's Fancy Dress party tonight at 6 p.m." he said formally.

Sarah looked quickly down at her watch pinned on to her dress. "But — but his costume?" she hadn't even given it a thought.

"We are supplying them, don't worry, Miss Danbury," trying to control a quivering lip.

The event proved to be a huge success, as most of the passengers were present, those who had been embarrassed, hoping that the culprits would get their just deserts. The boys filed in, every one trussed in white paper, only their eyes and shoes showing. One enterprising passenger later that evening at the adults' party, came with a chamberpot hanging around his neck and was delighted when he won a prize, because it was topical.

At the end of the children's party, Aunt Daphne and Sarah took, a very subdued Harry, back to his cabin, to release him, his mother gently chiding him all the while, but before he climbed up into his bunk, she hugged him. "Please Harry, no more larks. Please!" she pleaded.

"The ladies looked at us as if we were criminals," he muttered.

"You caused a lot of embarrassment and uncomfortableness to several people, Harry. Think about it. It was a very unkind prank."

"We'll be home tomorrow, Mama. I'll be glad," he said drowsily with a huge yawn, turned over and was soon asleep.

Later that evening Aunt Daphne and Sarah did not attend the adult Fancy Dress party, but after dinner attended the dance, Peter Fenn claiming Sarah, taking her for a stroll around the deck. "Miss Danbury, right through these last hours, you're been dreadfully downcast, why? Surely, what the boys did should have raised at least a smile?"

She shook her head. "I'm responsible for Harry Merton's actions and I failed. And whose idea was it to truss those children up like mummies? I would have thought, to open the lavatory doors, was punishment enough. Certain ladies would not have spared them."

"Oh, we did it for a lark, with the Captain's blessings." He hastened to add, seeing her strong disapproval, "I think branding his cat, did not help matters," he admitted truthfully. "You know, the last straw and all that?"

That night Aunt Daphne and Sarah retired to their cabins soon after ten o'clock. "My dear, you're going to bed early, why is that? I would have thought you and Mr. Fenn would have danced the night away."

Sarah shook her head. "I'm quite out of charity with him. Aunt Daphne, was

Harry so mischievous on your trip over to England?"

"No, I don't think so," she replied uncertainly, "but then Dirk, my other son, was with us and being a little older, is more responsible. Anyway, nothing drastic came to my ears."

"What can we say to him in the morning?"

"Nothing, Sarah dear," Aunt Daphne said comfortably. "He will come to us and say he's sorry and all will be forgiven. Having to open those doors and I'm sure there must have been someone there, will have been punishment enough."

Later, as Sarah lay on her bunk, she still could not laugh at what had happened. It was not likely that she would ever forget this trip. The Captain, at dinner, had again made reference to the outrage, with a stern admonition to the parents to keep their sons in better order, which she, herself, had taken to heart.

Harry had woken her early the next

morning and was soon on deck, the ship having docked sometime during the early hours, seagulls squabbling over the titbits thrown from junks and sampans that lined the wharf, as people began their day. There lay Hong Kong before her, amazed at the many solid block-like buildings which climbed up the huge mountain that seemed to tower over them.

The harbour was filled with a conglomeration of boats and ships laying at anchor. A British warship, and any number of clippers, lay peacefully cheek by jowl, the sun rising from above the hills that almost surrounded it. Now she could see why Aunt Daphne had said it was such a safe haven for shipping.

The bell rang for early breakfast and she went down to the diningroom where she found Aunt Daphne and Harry. Evidently there was no children's breakfast on the last morning.

"Thank goodness, we'll soon be home," said Aunt Daphne, as Sarah joined them, after greeting her, Harry urging her to hurry, so they might get into the queue.

When they eventually came up on deck with all their hand luggage, sailors carrying their trunks, it was to find that a great many people had arrived to welcome the ship. Aunt Daphne and Harry were eagerly looking out for Mr. Merton as they waited their turn to disembark, Sarah's gaze caught by a tall, fairhaired gentleman, sporting a beard, with every appearance of being a very successful man, the lady on his arm dressed in the very latest Parisian mode, a huge diamond on a gold chain, nestling in her plunging cleavage, her midnight black hair, falling in a shower of curls from under a hat that also spoke of that city, her eyes as blue as the seas they had just left behind. They made a striking couple.

Sarah was conscious of Aunt Daphne puckering up and wondered what had caused this, for she was the friendliest of souls.

"Ah, that's Simon Mac Gowan and Sophia Nedling. She's not *bon ton*, as far as I'm concerned," she murmured. "He's amassed his fortune from trade in tea, silks and opium, but it is said, that he only sold one consignment of opium, to set him up and has not dealt in it again. I see that she is still wig over buckles in love with him, or his wealth," to add inelegantly, "She won't be able to butter his paws, unless — unless something has happened while I've been away. How nice it is to be back and soon I shall hold a party. I've got to get up to date with all the news and dear, you may write out the invitations for me."

"Jason spoke of Mr. Mac Gowan, saying he was a clever, cunning man," to which Aunt Daphne agreed.

The gentleman's glance had met Sarah's interested one, his eyes narrowing, as he inclined his head. She was looking particularly fresh and young in an apricot muslin gown that complimented her tawny hair under a straw hat that Jason had given her at Malta, with ribbons to match.

Harry had, at that moment, caught sight of his father and started waving and shouting, Aunt Daphne's joyous face good to see, as she watched her husband squeezing his large frame through the mass of passengers, to grab both his wife and son, in a bearlike hug. It was a joy to see their loving reunion, Aunt Daphne a changed woman, coming alive at the sight of her husband.

Mr. Merton was introduced, saying how pleased he was that his wife had managed to find someone as pretty as Sarah, to help take care of Harry, who took instant exception to this, until Sarah raised an eyebrow, that called forth a cheeky grin from him, never doubting that his mother would keep silent as to what had happened on the trip, but his father would want to know from him.

Sarah took an instant liking to this large, jovial man and followed as he led the way down the gangway, his arm thrown across his son's shoulder, the other hand carrying one of the larger bags.

Just as Sarah was about to step on to solid earth again, she felt herself enveloped in a bearlike hug and swept off her feet, by a tall, lanky young man, with a shock of unruly red hair, knocking her hat askew, as kisses rained down on her surprised face.

"Oh, this is heaven to hold you again, my love, my love! The waiting has been unbearable," giving Sarah another squeeze and a smacking kiss. "We'll have the banns read from next Sunday," he said eagerly. "Oh, Agnes!" his voice with a quiver to it.

Sarah managed to tear herself away. "Please, Sir, I'm not Miss Picton," she said gently, to watch the joy drain from his expression, his pale blue eyes bleak.

His arms dropped to his sides as he peered into her face, to turn away abruptly, giving a gulp. "I suppose she met some other fellow and disembarked at Singapore? It happens."

She could only nod dumbly. "I'm so very sorry," she whispered, before hurrying to where the Mertons were standing, who had witnessed the whole scene, helpless.

"What a dreadful shock for poor Dick," murmured Aunt Daphne, on the verge of tears.

"I knew young Forbes was expecting his fiance and Daphne has told me all about his Agnes; my sympathies go out to him," said Mr. Merton, to suggest seriously, "I would deem it a help, Miss Danbury if you would console that young man, as I couldn't possibly bear with him in the coming weeks. He's in my department, you know," and hailed three rickshaws. The luggage was loaded into one and the others used by the family and away they went, amid much laughter, Sarah delighted by this mode of transport.

"I'm so thrilled Harry, to be in Hong Kong," noticing a three-masted junk leaving the harbour, with its high forecastle and fluted rust coloured sails. "Now I know I'm in the Far East and, of course, because of all the Chinese people."

The rickshaws drew up in front of a large, double storied, flat roofed house, a high wall surrounding the property, the iron gate being opened by a white haired old man, who grinned broadly as he welcomed home his Mistress and Master Harry.

Mr. Merton helped his wife down, Harry giving Sarah a hand, Aunt Daphne saying with heartfelt relief, "Oh for a bed that doesn't dip and sway!" and sighed pleasurably at the very thought.

She introduced the old butler to Sarah. "Briggs, Miss Danbury very kindly, at the last moment, agreed to accompany me and was a great help, as you well can imagine."

Briggs bowed, before leading them all into the drawing-room, saying that tea would be served, immediately.

"We just had to bring Briggs with us," explained Aunt Daphne, seating her self, "and bless him, he was quite willing to come with us to a foreign land."

Without waiting for tea, Harry excused himself before dashing off to be reunited with his dog and to see if his hedgehog had survived.

5

SARAH followed Aunt Daphne into a fair sized drawing-room, a lived in room she was quick to note, with several comfy sofas upholstered in pinks and blues, easy chairs and a large display cabinet that held many charming pieces of Eastern pottery.

As for Aunt Daphne, she was a different person, smiling at her employer who read her thoughts accurately. "My dear, I'm always out of curl when I'm away from my husband," she said simply, with a fond glance at him. "It has never been a hardship to live here, although some wives dislike the country so much who, after long leave, just don't return. So sad when families break up."

Tea was brought in by a smiling Chinese maid, introduced as Mei-mei, who bobbed a curtsy, Aunt Daphne asking, "You talky, talky Master Harry, he come downside quick quick," and as the maid left the room, "I've taught Mei-mei to smile and laugh, no inscrutable Chinese in my house, thank you!"

Sarah caught Mr. Merton's amused gaze. "Pidgin English," seeing her incomprehension. "And all Chinese surnames are spoken first," he explained kindly.

It was also clear that he was delighted to have his family back and began to enquire about his eldest son, very concerned as to whether he had settled down at his new school, or not.

"I suppose we must just wait for Dirk's first letter, my love," soothed his wife, who hid her own concern.

At that moment a small white and black dog shot into the room, to greet Aunt Daphne hysterically, scattering the rugs on the highly polished wood floor, uttering yelps of delight, until Harry calmed him down.

After tea, Mr. Merton excused himself, saying he had to get back to the office, leaving the ladies to unpack and his wife to take up the reins of her household again.

William Merton was a gentlemanly man, a little too conscious, perhaps, of his high position in Government, but a very pleasant man, for all that.

Sarah was taken upstairs, where she was shown into a pretty room that was furnished with floral cotton curtains, that were blowing in the breeze, a beautifully carved Chinese kist across one corner.

"Sarah, please don't drink the water. There is always cold tea available. I'm afraid our water is suspect, even though we have our own well."

Sarah nodded. "Aunt Daphne, are you really happy and contented living here in this far flung British colony?"

"Like many others here, dear, we watch our pennies and dream of a own home in Britain when William retires, but yes, I really enjoy living here and

221

so does William, except of course, that our sons will have to attend school in Britain, but thank goodness, I'm back on terra firma again," to give a heartfelt sigh. "Now I'm ready to hold a party for my friends and get up to date with all their news and any new scandal."

"I'm due to catch the next ship back home, remember?" joining her employer on the window seat, who smiled at her kindly.

"Sarah dear, I hope that you'll be willing to stay a while."

"Harry will be at school, most of the day. I can't be of much help now," she pointed out.

"Oh, but I'd like you to stay and is there any urgency to go back? Really, I mean. I'm sure the hospital will always accept you," she coaxed.

There was a pause, Aunt Daphne eyeing her expectantly, until Sarah smilingly agreed. "Thank you, but I'll not expect to be paid," she said firmly. "My brother gave me sufficient money to pay for my simple needs."

"Very well, dear," acceding gracefully, "but I do so want to introduce you to our English community and for you to join in our festivities," seating herself more comfortably. "I've been thinking that we should keep up the charade of you being the daughter of a dear friend of mine. You had a disappointment — " Sarah giving her a startled glance. This was too close to the truth for her liking, one that Aunt Daphne fortunately, had failed to notice. "And I came up with the suggestion that a sea trip would set you up, nicely. It worked on the boat," seeing Sarah's doubts, "and will work equally well here," she said firmly. "You'll also have a chance of meeting several eligible young gentlemen and who knows?" archly, swishing out of the room before Sarah could reply.

As she made her way downstairs again, she felt as if she had matured considerably, because now, her destiny lay in her own hands. No more would she have to stay with Bertram and

Louise. It was an exhilarating thought that drew a satisfied glance from her hostess.

"Ah, Sarah, just in time for luncheon," rising to her feet. "So nice to be in my own home again and not feel guilty when I give an order. My sister-in-law is a dear, but one is never really comfortable except in one's own home. Anyway, that's what I've found."

Luncheon was a simple meal of baked fish and vegetables with a fruit pie to follow.

Mr. Merton arrived back home later that afternoon and it was evident that it was his custom at this time of day to pour himself a glass of wine, while Aunt Daphne and Sarah took tea, Harry chatting away. After the news of the day had been shared, Mr. Merton was allowed to read the *China Mail* at his leisure, until dinner was served at an early hour. A pleasant meal of curried chicken, pancakes, vegetables and, once again, fruit, Aunt Daphne mentioning that their guest was to delay her return, Mr. Merton and Harry of the opinion, that she would be very welcome.

"You might as well," said Mr. Merton kindly, "now you are here. Sarah, I would deem it a favour, if you would take young Dick in hand and soothe his lacerated feelings. Please!" this was an urgent plea for help, that Sarah could not ignore and agreed, albeit a little apprehensibly.

Harry excused himself, not interested in grownup talk, leaving Mr. Merton to add with marked concern. "Dick wasn't at work today," turning to his wife. "I've decided to send a courier to Singapore to look into this matter of Miss Picton's non arrival."

Startled, Aunt Daphne frowned. "But — but, William, do you think she would thank you for that?" she asked uncertainly.

"What kind of girl, is she?"

"Simple, pretty and very young for her age," she replied.

"All the more reason to try and

rescue her," he insisted. "I wouldn't
have a moment's peace, not knowing
if that child was safe. And, my
dear, please invite Dick to your next
party. There is also another young
man, Hector Carew, who was highly
recommended by London. He was in
our Calcutta office, arriving here while
you were away. He's about thirty, I
would say, and would appreciate an
invitation, I'm sure. He's in a boarding
house, at present."

"What is he like?" his wife wanted
to know.

"Brown hair, blue eyes, a little taller
than I am and very quiet."

"Like a whole lot of other men," she
replied with a twinkle. "Of course, I'll
include him on my list, dear."

Later that night, Sarah thankfully
tumbled into bed, blessedly stationery
and wide awake, thinking how pleasantly
she had spent the weeks on board ship,
to fall asleep immediately.

The following morning she awoke to
another pleasant day, Mei-mei bringing

in a can of hot water and a cup of China tea, to say that Master Harry had gone to 'talky, talky listen', which Sarah supposed, was school, returning the maid's cheerful grin, refusing her offer to help her get dressed, Mei-mei's straight black hair cut just below her ears, her fringe touching her eyebrows, reminding Sarah of the doll she had had as a small child.

She dressed quickly and went downstairs to find Aunt Daphne just finishing her tea, in *déshabillé* in a frilly robe of the finest apricot silk.

"Aunt Daphne, good morning, I'm dreadfully sorry I'm late. I'll know in future," she excused herself.

"My dear, I always have breakfast with my husband. It's a nice way to start the day, we think."

Sarah's smile was sunny. "You are fast teaching me what a loving marriage should be," Mei-mei coming in at that moment with her breakfast of baked fish, onions and cheese and a fresh rack of toast, giving her a choice of either tea or claret. All the meals had been a welcome change from what she was used to, refreshingly different and remarked on this.

"We have to make do with what we can get," was the simple reply.

After the breakfast table had been cleared, Aunt Daphne reached for a file, to take out a list of names. "This party I wish to hold, will be held in three days' time which will give all my friends the opportunity to welcome me back," Sarah hiding a smile at this high-handedness and offered to write out all the invitations.

"Sarah, thank you. I'll accept that offer gratefully," and began going through the list of names and addresses, coming at last, to the name of Simon Mac Gowan, to tell her more about this gentleman.

He's one of the top ten most successful businessmen, *tai-pans*, in the Far East. Remember I pointed him out to you yesterday morning, that tall gentleman, who was with that overdressed young woman?"

Sarah's head came up quickly to nod. "*Tai-Pan*?" she murmured, savouring the word on the tip of her tongue.

"It is the name given to the Supreme Leader, the one who wields the power. Simon Mac Gowan is one such in his own trading company, here in Hong Kong," and with that bustled out of the room, to pause at the door. "Our groom will deliver those invitations as soon as you have finished them and I'll be excused for inviting the guests at such short notice. Oh, and please add Dick's name and also that of Hector Carew."

Sarah suddenly noticed her name on the list and queried it.

"Aunt Daphne, do you think it is wise to foist me on to Hong Kong society? If it ever became common knowledge that I was a mere paid companion, what would your friends say?"

"Nonsense!" Aunt Daphne sounding unusually firm. "No one will ever find out and you did a sterling job," she said comfortingly, to run on. "I must say this again, I'm much obliged to you, Sarah, for giving up your nursing career to accompany me home. I don't know what I'd have done without you and you minded Harry splendidly — " Sarah giving a grimace, that Aunt Daphne chose to ignore, "and nursed me through that awful bout of seasickness," shuddering at the very thought. "My child, I don't want another chirp out of you re this matter and now, here you are acting as my secretary. I also want you to meet our eligible young gentlemen — "

Sarah did not catch the rest of the sentence, for Aunt Daphne had hurried from the room.

Sunday arrived, Dick Forbes presenting himself just as the family were leaving for church, asking if he could spend the day with them.

"I — I don't know how I would have gone on by myself," he said gratefully, as both his hosts smiled an acceptance, his eyes going to Sarah, who was looking a picture this morning in a blue muslin, her small hat lined with the same material, her smile sympathetically kind.

The family carriage stopped outside St. John's Cathedral, which, Dick said importantly, was inaugurated in 1849 and was built in the shape of a cross, as many cathedrals were.

The bells had stopped chiming, as the family entered; Sarah could have been back in the church her family attended and was strangely comforted. Priscilla could have been sitting next to her, her treble out trebling the choir boys. Suddenly, she was a little homesick, all this so dearly familiar, wondering how her niece was doing at the School for Young Ladies. There was a difference though, a large portion of the congregation was Chinese. After the service, Mrs. Merton invited Dick to spend the rest of the day with them, which he gladly accepted and after luncheon, Mr. Merton suggested that they take Sarah sightseeing, once again Briggs acting as coachman, Dick, this time managing to seat himself next to Sarah, Harry glaring at him. As they drove through the streets, they were stopped many times by friends, welcoming back Aunt Daphne, asking if they might be introduced to her very pretty friend, Sarah surprised and gratified by this mark of respect.

As they passed the Post Office, Aunt Daphne suggested they show Sarah the impressive Mac Gowan's Emporium, that she noticed, would not have disgraced the best London could offer.

The Square was filled with people taking the air. Decorous English families, many men in uniform; young children and their Chinese nursemaids and ladies in dainty dresses and bonnets, some walking, others driven by liveried coachmen. Sarah also noticed that most men wore tussore suits and cotton shirts, Mr. Merton himself, choosing this mode of dress, presumedly because of the hot weather.

To round off the afternoon drive, Briggs drove them to the bottom of Victoria Peak, where Sarah was told that one could go up the very steep incline in either a sedan chair, or walk, Dick quick to suggest that he would like to escort her. This was a new area being opened up, several mansions in prime positions, were either occupied, or were in the process of being built.

On their way home, they passed a Chinese pagoda, its roof of brightly coloured, shiny porcelain tiles, the corners turned up to the sun, made a charming picture, the garden a mass of many hued flowers.

"This must surely belong to a fairy tale," Sarah murmured, entranced.

Aunt Daphne agreed. "I also like pagodas." At that moment two high-born Chinese ladies came into view, beautifully gowned, their faces painted masks. Briggs had slowed down the carriage and Sarah had a view of their long finger nails, encased in gold sheaths.

"How can they do anything," she asked in amazement.

"They don't work, neither do they spin," replied Mr. Merton dryly. "Everything is done for them and if those nails weren't encased, they would curl around."

"Father, they would be lovely to scratch their husbands' backs with," piped up Harry.

Even Dick chuckled, very gratified that he was sitting next to this beautiful young lady, for a moment Agnes forgotten.

Sarah sank back against the seat, with a sigh. "I'm very impressed. Hong Kong is such a thriving country, but my brother did say that there were people who were not pleased at the take over. It looks a roaring success."

"Yes," replied Dick eagerly. "Nobody then saw the potential for British trade here and that is what has made Hong Kong so successful."

Mr. Merton sitting opposite, raised an eyebrow. "You surprise me, Dick.

There's hope for you, yet," he said with patient resignation.

"Well, dash it all, Sir," indignantly. "If the fate of this land of ours had been left in certain bigwigs' hands, China would be in control now. Anyone could have seen it, if they had any sense in their cocklofts. What cakes they made of themselves! Poor things," adding simply, in a fair minded way, "they weren't here."

The evening of Aunt Daphne's party was upon them, the house ablaze with light, Briggs kept busy ushering in the guests, who warmly welcomed her back. Their community was such, that even one member was sorely missed. Sarah was introduced.

"Always nice to welcome new people to Hong Kong, Miss Danbury," every one said, until Sarah began to feel guilty, her old bogy back.

Several guests had not been able to attend, having prior engagements, Hector Carew amongst them.

Simon Mac Gowan, however did

arrive, much to Aunt Daphne's gratification, introducing Sarah, who wondered if this gentleman was one of the eligibles, whom Aunt Daphne had mentioned. She was looking particularly summery in a pale green silk, embroidered with silver wheatears.

As the musical part of the evening progressed, Dick sitting next to her, became more and more annoyed at the way Mr. Gowan was eyeing his partner, Sarah herself a little uneasy. It was not *comme il faut* and tilted her chin at him, but when the dancing commenced, he approached her to beg her pardon, with an amused glint in his pale blue eyes, saying that his thoughts had been elsewhere. Excusing himself, Dick walked off in disgust.

Mr. Mac Gowan talked for a while, keeping Sarah entertained with stories of some of his sailing experiences in his deep voice, traces of his Scottish ancestry still evident, before asking her to dance with him.

He was a tall, lithe person, with a

body tutored in a life of hardship, his skin deeply tanned by the elements. He had come to his high position in the business world the hard way, now enjoying the fruit of his labours, his business being that of textiles and tea. He also owned a fleet of clippers, buying tea from China, the proceeds funding his many enterprises, but had not yet reached the zenith of his ambitions, that of *Tai-Pan* of *tai-pans*.

As Sarah danced with him, she really began to enjoy herself, for he was a superb dancer.

He broke a silence with, "How delightful to meet a newcomer to our small colony, Miss Danbury, an English rose no less and how well your gown suits those eyes and that tawny topknot; our ladies will be extremely envious of that peach blossom skin, Miss Danbury," guiding her expertly through a knot of dancers.

"Why, thank you, *Tai-Pan*," the words mysterious, evocative.

He was amused at the far away expression that had crept into her eyes.

"I think you like my title?" he murmured cynically.

"It belongs to the realm of fairyland," she said dreamily.

"Nothing so unsubstantial as that," his reply dry. "It has taken years of hard work and bargaining to get where I have got to," a little indignant.

"Are you making a long stay, Miss Danbury?" his voice cool.

"I don't think so," her reply equally disinterested. "I have responsibilities back home. Aunt Daphne has been most kind, asking me to stay on for a little while longer, as we get on so very well."

"You'll be welcome in Hong Kong, as there is a predominance of unmarried males here. I presume Daphne has marriage in mind for you?" interested in her reply.

Sarah was experienced enough to turn aside this innuendo, but he sensed her sudden coolness.

"And what business is that of yours, *Tai-Pan*?" she asked quietly, as he swung her around again, his hand firm on her back.

He chuckled, suddenly amused. "I now have a mission to see those cool green eyes of yours soften." The music had stopped and with a bow, took her back to Aunt Daphne. "How interesting," he murmured in her ear. "Now I'll leave you to young Dick, who is green with envy, assuaging the loss of his lady love?"

The next dance was a Strauss polka, which Dick and Sarah turned into a mad romp, the younger guests joining in the fun, Aunt Daphne beaming at their enthusiasm. Some time later Sarah noticed that Mr. Mac Gowan had left, to leave her wondering why he had even condescended to attend. Was it in deference to his hostess?

As the last guest left, Aunt Daphne slumped into an easy chair, kicking off her shoes and ordering tea. "Well, the evening was a success, I think," with a gusty sigh. "Sarah, thank you for all your support. I saw you chatting to several of the older ladies."

She nodded. "I found Jane and Esmeralda Finch particularly interesting. They have been teachers in several countries, such as Australia, New Zealand and India and have a fund of fascinating stories. I enjoyed their chatter immensely," she said tiredly, barely able to keep her eyes open.

"We're very fortunate in having them in our English school. Miss Jane helped Dirk a great deal this last year, enabling him to enter Eton," giving another huge yawn. "I think, dear, it's time you sought your bed."

Mr. Merton bade Sarah a kindly 'goodnight' to add, "The sooner I receive an answer about Agnes, the better it will be for all of us. That young cub should have his ears trimmed, the way he acted tonight and thank you, m'dear, for bearing with his jealousy."

"Mr. Merton, I feel desperately sorry for him and I didn't mind, at all."

"People are going to think that Sarah has a beau," Aunt Daphne, gurgled.

"Nonsense, Daphne!" said her husband crossly, Sarah taking the opportunity to slip away to her bed.

Mr. Merton also talked to his wife about Hector Carew. "I'm worried about that young man too, Daphne. There must have been some tragedy in his life. I wish that he had come tonight."

As for the *tai-pan*, his thoughts were all on Sarah and her unconscious charm, his senses stirring.

The days passed pleasantly, Sarah being accepted by the small English community and had attended several morning teas and evening functions, amazed that she could have been in any home, her brother and Louise visited, the only difference being, that the servants were Chinese.

The weather had cooled down a little, but even so, all the calls were still made in the mornings.

"Most ladies sleep in the afternoon,"

explained Aunt Daphne, "I very often do the same myself, for the mid summer heat is excessive and enervating and one quickly falls into the habit, which I find relaxing."

The following morning, Aunt Daphne suggested that Sarah go exploring on her own. "I've a committee meeting that I really must attend. It is one of my favourite charities, that of schooling for Chinese children, the other being the stopping of women, binding babies' feet. This practise, I'm glad to say, is dying out. The rule, however, does not apply to peasant babies, for who would then gather in the harvests," her observation cynical.

"But why should their feet be bound? They must grow dreadfully deformed and the pain for those poor little dears must be unendurable. It's — it's too ghastly to think of," Sarah aghast at this inhumanity.

"It's the Chinese men. It's a sexual thing with them," she accused with loathing, lowering her voice, quickly changing the subject, as Sarah was about to put another question.

"Mei-mei will, of course, accompany you. She'll appreciate time off from her chores and it's a beautiful morning," suggesting Sarah visit the flower market. "It is worth seeing and we do need flowers for the drawing-room."

Sarah and Mei-mei, however, decided not to walk, but hired instead, two sedan chairs, with pretty floral curtains, Mei-mei giggling and gesticulating, trying to tell her to hang on to the sides. However, Sarah, not understanding, was thrown back, quite roughly, when the two men suddenly, picked up the chair and placed the shafts on their shoulders, Mei-mei convulsed with laughter.

They did not have far to travel and were soon set down at the flower market, Mei-mei walking decorously some distance back from Sarah, who was fascinated by all the different flowers on offer, most of them having been brought in from Nanking, only a few having been grown in the hinterland. "I shall buy myself a nosegay," she promised herself, but it was difficult to choose, a little startled when a gentleman came up behind her to say, "Perhaps I could be of some help, Miss Danbury?"

She turned around, recognising Simon Mac Gowan, astonished that he should notice her, giving him a quick smile. "Good morning, *Tai-Pan*. Isn't this a lovely bower of flowers?" noticing that he was impeccably dressed, the picture of a successful business man, his cravat tastefully arranged and swinging a malacca cane, in a very debonair fashion. He appeared older somehow, this morning, the strong sun not kindly to his harsh face, his eyes though, paid tribute to her simple muslin gown and colourful Japanese paper sunshade, which she was using to good effect.

"May I be of some service to you, Miss Danbury, perhaps carrying your flowers home? And I must add that you are looking very pretty this morning?"

he said with a bow.

"No thank you, *Tai-Pan*, the *amah* is not too far away," acknowledging the compliment, so eloquent of incredulity that he was taken aback, but made a recovery.

"I do like your hat and being an owner of a large apparel emporium, I'm naturally interested in where you purchased it."

"Someone bought it for me during our stop in Malta, Sir," demurely.

"Ah, a gentleman, I presume?"

She nodded, "And he happens to know you, *Tai Pan*," amused, as she recalled what Jason had said about him.

"Might I know the name of this gentleman?" showing some interest.

"A Mr. Jason Goodall, do you remember him?"

"Ah, the man from Forsythe's, yes indeed! That was an epic battle which I won, naturally."

"He called you a clever, cunning man," she added, taking exception to his boastful manner, "but, I suppose, you take that as a compliment?"

"That young gentlemen must also learn these attributes, if he desires success here in the Far East," he said dryly.

"Very fitting, *Tai-Pan*, your lion and bear being your opponents, I presume?" she retorted sweetly.

He was surprised into an attractive, boyish grin. "I'm no David, Miss Sarah," offering her his arm, which she took, her gaze still intent on the mass of colour surrounding her.

No one, for some time, had dared to take him to task like this and strangely enough, he rather liked it, as most women in his life had never had the spunk to disagree with him. Knowing Sarah was quite an experience for him, finding he was much attracted to Daphne's little friend.

"May I walk with you, or is this your only destination?"

Sarah nodded happily. "Aunt Daphne suggested I come here this morning to buy flowers for the house, as she has a committee meeting."

"A lady of good deeds is our Daphne," he approved, suddenly realising and intrigued that he had received no melting looks from her and his interest increased, stopping at a display of orchids, to buy several sprays, presenting them to Sarah, with a bow.

"How beautiful they are," she murmured. "My thanks, *Tai-Pan*."

They reached the end of the street and the flower market. She turned to him. "This is where I leave you," looking up at him with a smile. At that moment the noonday gun was suddenly fired and Sarah jumped, then chuckled. "I still haven't become used to that," she confessed, beckoning Mei-mei to join her, Sarah taking some of the flowers, holding out her hand to that gentleman, which he kissed.

"You rival those blooms you are holding, Miss Sarah," his eyes appreciating her dainty beauty. He hailed two chairs, giving direction to the men. As he was about to help Sarah into the chair, a carriage drew up, seated in it was the black haired, full-figured beauty, whom she had noticed on the wharf, the day she had arrived; Sophia Nedling.

The lady ignored her, asking sweetly, if Simon required a lift. He nodded, to turn to help Sarah into the chair, standing back to watch her go, before mounting the carriage, asking the coachman to drop him off at his place of business.

Sophia was greatly put out when she realised that Simon was disinclined to talk, in fact ignoring her. Was it Sarah Danbury who was the cause of this silence?

Simon's thoughts were elsewhere, conscious of a feeling of dissatisfaction, which was quite foreign to him.

The carriage stopped, but as he was about to step down, Sophia placed a hand on his sleeve and whispered something which made his eyebrows fly up in surprise, but made no comment, except to wish her a 'good day'.

What he had just learned, put a different aspect on matters, his brow clearing.

Latterly, he had been thinking of marriage, as he had to have an heir who would eventually, take over his vast business concerns when he retired. He would, of course, marry into the aristocracy and such was his high opinion of himself, that this was a decided possibility. He would choose a wife, the daughter of a duke, who would be able to introduce him to the best in British society, but he found, rather to his chagrin, that Sarah pulled at his heartstrings.

He could never marry her, of course, for what Sophia had just whispered to him, was that she was only a paid companion of Daphne's and not the daughter of a dear friend. He smiled and fingered his beard, thinking of all the items of apparel he would shower on her and jewels from all over the world and what woman could resist such an offer?

When Sarah arrived back at the house, she related what had occurred, Aunt Daphne pleased that she was meeting people, especially Simon Mac Gowan, she said archly, to which Sarah retorted indignantly, "I like his Chinese name, that's all. It trips off my tongue, quite delightfully."

Because of the smallness of the English community, folk tended to mind each other's business and if a gentleman showed even the slightest interest in a lady, wedding bells were forecast, so when someone had seen the *Tai-Pan* with Miss Sarah Danbury, the news was quickly circulated. What a feather in her cap, thought Aunt Daphne gleefully, if Simon Mac Gowan would propose to her erstwhile companion.

The days passed pleasantly, Sarah very much at home in the community, most people, by now, aware that she was to take up a nursing career, as soon as she returned to Britain, determined to follow in dear Florence Nightingale's footsteps.

Sarah was, however, still very uneasy about the fib that had been started by Aunt Daphne, oh, with the very best of intentions, but what if someone found out that she had been a paid companion and nothing more? She cringed at the very thought and had spoken to Aunt Daphne about this again, but she had, once more, brushed it aside in her airy fashion.

* * *

Hector Carew had travelled around extensively during the last five years, mostly due to the Foreign Office, working in various countries in the far flung British empire and had been sent to take up a position in the Hong Kong government several months ago. Prior to this posting, he had been in the Calcutta office and was pleased with the change. For reasons only known to himself, he had not accepted many invitations, but rather took work home to his hotel rooms, where he was comfortably housed.

He was a well built young man in his late twenties, with dark hair and deep blue eyes and a very pleasant manner. Tired of flirting, yet adverse to considering marriage, he found himself at an impasse, wondering what would be his eventual fate, probably ending up as an old crotchety bachelor.

His gloomy forebodings were, however, lightened somewhat, when he was asked to go out on the north road to get a progress report on a new bridge under construction, also to try and obtain a date from the engineers as to when the bridge would be completed, for the lack of one, was holding back the opening of this area.

Hector was on his way back to the office, when he suddenly drew his horses to a halt. A little way ahead, was a young lady who had stopped suddenly, as a white, frilly garment slithered to her feet. He was about to jump down, but she was already calmly stepping out of the offending garment, folded it neatly and placed it, nonchalantly, over her arm.

His mouth twitched, a deep throaty chuckle escaping him, as he picked up the reins again, but held the horses, as he caught sight of Simon Mac Gowan approach the lady, taking her arm and walking away with her. He frowned. Ha! lay the wind in that direction? The *tai-pan* was no fit companion for such a young girl and decided that he would, from now on, attend the island's social functions more often as he resumed his journey, another chuckle bubbling out. It had been a refreshing interlude.

Sarah had naturally, been extremely embarrassed and that it was Simon Mac Gowan who had witnessed her predicament, his eyes lazily amused by the mishap, as he asked if he could be of some assistance.

"Certainly not, Mr. Mac Gowan and it would have been more gentlemanly if you had ignored the whole incident," glaring at him and continued to walk away.

He followed her, stopping in front of a stall that contained a wide choice of fans and bought one, presenting it to her saying that it was a very hot day, no hint of the amusement he felt, at her high colour.

It was a beautiful one, a scatter of flowers painted on ivory, Sarah accepting it, her eyes sparkling mischievously over it's top, the old Chinese shaking his head, as he watched the couple stroll away. In his culture only the very highborn ones wore beautiful clothes, the lower classes wore baggy grey trousers and shirts, but found himself appreciating the pretty colours in the lady's dress and her green eyes, that reminded him of his small garden, which he cultivated on his tiny piece of flat earth.

"Miss Sarah, you're still calling me by my title. I have a wish to hear my christian name on your lips."

"I'll not call you anything else, Sir, for the words sing of far places, they're music — " stopping, a little annoyed with herself, by this rhetoric, asking that he call a chair for her.

"Why the hurry?" he asked easily. "Come, let's enjoy a walk on the promenade," and took her arm, to arrive at the sea front, where they found seats, Sarah sinking down with a sigh of pure happiness.

"I'm so glad I have been given this opportunity to visit this lovely colony and I'll be sorry to leave."

"Don't you think we could dispense with the *amah*?" he suggested, catching sight of Mei-mei a little way from them. "I'd like to escort you home, Miss Sarah."

Sarah shook her head. "Aunt Daphne would be most displeased, *Tai-Pan*."

"But Daphne is not your aunt, is she? You are just a paid companion," with a lifted eyebrow.

She inclined her head. "Yes," she admitted, "but my wages stopped when I stepped into Aunt Daphne's house and I'm only staying on for a while, at her invitation. Aunt Daphne, bless her, is an extremely bad traveller and I was very glad that I could be of some help and Harry — well! I certainly earned my wages, believe you me. "I have felt uncomfortable about the lie I've had to live, but it was at her suggestion."

"So you scorn to dissemble, I like that and in these days, is rare," quizzing her.

"I can't say the same about you. *Tai-Pan*, you've been snooping and didn't think you could stoop so low," not mincing her words or her accusing tone.

He shrugged, a little taken aback. "I must admit I'm interested in you, Miss Sarah. Can you blame me? I enjoy your zest for life and you're very beautiful. Will you come away with me?"

No words came to her aid this time, as she looked at him in shocked astonishment, *mistress*, hanging in the air like wisps of fog. "A *carte blanche*?" she squeaked. "How dare you!" her cheeks pink with outrage.

"Please Miss Sarah, remember where

we are," trying to calm her, ignoring her angry eyes, wondering how he would deal with a fit of the vapours, but she was only coldly vexed.

"I'm behaving very well," she snapped. "No thanks to you, Mr. Mac Gowan."

"Perhaps, you are a little upset, but there can be no question of marriage, my dear. I'll set you up very comfortably and though I'll be away from time to time, my business as you know, takes me far and wide, I'll supply you with an *amah*, to keep you company," he promised coolly.

Sarah kept her head averted, hiding the hurt disbelief but managed to say, with forced disappointment, "Oh, won't you take me on one of your lovely clippers?"

He smiled to himself. Sarah would come around to his way of thinking. He had kept a fancy piece or two in his time, as some men did, but had never trifled with well bred young women, but Sarah was, after all, only someone who had to earn her bread and butter, but was surprised by her mundane question.

"Why yes, of course I will. You could accompany me, where ever I might travel, India, Japan, China — "

"But I would not be able to live in Hong Kong?"

"No," the answer bald and unequivocal. "I'll give you a beautiful home, which shall be yours when, one day we should part company, as I suppose we will. I'm not tight-fisted and will see that your future is secured," he assured her with calm sang froid.

Sarah was suddenly afraid. Could this man abduct her and shivered. No, he could never do that for he had too high a standing in this country, nevertheless, she gave a quick glance around. There stood Mei-mei, bless her, patiently waiting for her. What a silly fear and relaxed again. She must appear normal, for there were too many people sauntering past, enjoying the sea breezes. She could not walk away either, denying the urge to give him the trimming of his life. Her cold gaze never wavered from his face, her bearing that of an outraged duchess and suddenly the *tai-pan* felt a stirring of misgiving. Had he made a ghastly mistake and watched her mulish expression. Was this little English rose going to refuse a *tai-pan*'s offer? Not likely, he thought cynically.

"Mr. Mac Gowan — " he was quick to notice this formal address, "What a coldblooded arrangement you have just offered me. You feel nothing for me, or I you. How could any such liaison work?" not able to control the shudder that ran through her.

"You do have to work for your living, Miss Sarah and your life under my protection, would be far easier," he argued reasonably, stifling a chuckle. Who would have thought this girl had such fire in her. What a pleasure it would be to tame that fire, until he could partake of its warmth.

"You would not have made me this offer, if I had really been the daughter of Aunt Daphne's friend," lowering her eyes. "And what would this English community and the Merton's say if I disappeared on board one of your clippers?"

"You'll catch a boat back to England, where I'll meet you," he replied coolly.

Her eyes met his again, not hiding the loathing she felt for him. "I decline your unflattering offer, Mr. Mac Gowan," and at that moment, all her ancestors stood at her back, her stare regal as she rose to her feet unhurriedly, to offer her *pièce de résistance*. "I much prefer a nursing career and I have a dream of my own. Good day to you, Simon Mac Gowan," stripping him of his title again. "This is one business transaction you have lost."

He caught her arm. "Nursing?" For the first time in his life, the *Tai-Pan* was completely taken aback. "A life of drudgery, under awful conditions! Nursing! You mean you'd choose that instead of a life under my care and everything I could give you?" words at last, failing him.

She nodded, turning away, but he again detained her. "If you won't be my mistress, would you consider becoming a model in my firm?"

Sarah did not deign to reply walking away, Mr. Mac Gowan staring at her retreating figure, but she suddenly stiffened, for from behind her came a bellow of laughter.

He watched her go. "Phew! She looked at me as if I'd just crawled out from under a stone," leaving him with a great deal to think over. "Well, laddie, you've bungled badly this time. Pluck up, she'll change her mind," but he could not forget what had happened. Even though he wouldn't admit it, Miss Danbury's rejection of him, was a crushing blow to his pride, but from the ashes, there grew a feeling that this girl meant more to him than he thought possible. Who would have thought that young Miss could have given him such a setdown. He stopped in his stride, a disquieting thought making him wonder who she really was. He shrugged and made his way back to his office.

Sarah and Mei-mei walked back home in silence, until the Chinese girl murmured sympathetically, guessing what had happened. "*Tai-Pan* not good. You talky talky Mr. Merton?"

"No, no! I won't worry him," but did wonder why Aunt Daphne hadn't warned her about Mr. Mac Gowan. Perhaps she didn't know.

It was in the same angry mood that Sarah entered the house, thankful that Aunt Daphne was out and went up to her bedroom, ignoring Mr. Brigg's greeting, Mei-mei chattering away in Mandarin to the old butler, who had picked up the language, over the years, that Miss was very upset.

Once in her room, Sarah slammed the door, allowing her anger full reign, throwing herself on to the bed. "How could he have thought I was that type of girl," she stormed. "I've never been so insulted in my life!" and promptly burst into tears.

She heard Aunt Daphne return, washed her face, redid her hair and went downstairs again to find it was time for luncheon.

"You look a little under the weather, Sarah dear," passing her a bowl of fruit salad.

"I do feel a little tired, Aunt Daphne," but that didn't satisfy the lady, wanting to know what parts of the town she had visited and whom she had met.

Sarah complied, saying that she had lost her petticoat and that Mr. Mac Gowan had bought her a pretty fan.

Aunt Daphne commiserated, with a smile. "You should be honoured by that gentleman's attentions."

"Should I, Aunt Daphne?"

"You're a very strange young lady," she said with exasperation, but changed the subject much to Sarah's relief.

One early afternoon, soon after

Sarah's disastrous meeting with the *Tai-Pan*, she entered the drawing-room to find that gentleman, sitting with Aunt Daphne, lounging elegantly, one leg over the other, but rose quickly as she entered, indignant at his effrontery, much to that gentleman's lazy amusement. He was wearing buckskin breeches, top boots and a scarf tied carelessly around his throat and was far more relaxed.

"Ah, my dear, there you are! Did you enjoy your walk?" Aunt Daphne enquired brightly.

"I was only feeding Harry's hedgehog."

Mr. Briggs knocked to ask if their guest required any refreshment, the tightening of his lips conveying plainly, what he thought of this man. The offer was declined and he withdrew in a stately manner.

"Simon has extended an invitation to take you sailing this afternoon, dear. In one of his clippers," adding with a pleased smile, that Sarah viewed with misgivings, a nasty chilly feeling in her stomach and smitten to silence.

"I don't think it would be — " she finally managed to say, signalling her doubts, which were ignored.

Simon met her stormy eyes, with a look of bland innocence, guessing that she had not told Daphne about his reprehensible proposal. What a fool he had been, not to have recognised her quality.

"My carriage is an open one, Miss Danbury," his smile one of sympathy, guessing exactly what her feelings were and at the same time, approving of the pretty sea-green voile dress, that matched her eyes, exactly.

"Simon has suggested you take Mei-mei and I'm in agreement," Aunt Daphne hastened to add, conscious of Sarah's swift withdrawal. "It will be perfectly in order, dear. Go and enjoy the afternoon. You have my blessing."

"It would give me great pleasure, Miss Danbury, to show you over one of my clippers and for you to experience the swiftness of one of them, under your feet."

"Thank you, Mr. Mac Gowan," she replied woodenly. There was nothing more she could say in the face of Aunt Daphne's approbation, but experienced a nervous qualm that she fought down, the good manners that had been instilled in her from childhood, helping to keep a still tongue in her head.

The gentleman bowed, with exaggerated grace, his eyes gleaming with amusement, as she flounced from the room, much to Aunt Daphne's surprise. She would have thought Sarah would welcome the idea of sailing with Simon, hoping that would remove the cloud which so often crept across her features when she thought no one was observing her.

"Don't forget to pack your largest hatpin," he called out, as Sarah disappeared through the door, to hear Aunt Daphne say,

"Simon, you'll look after the child? She's become like a daughter to me."

Sarah dressed with haste, Mei-mei

excited that she was to go too, helping Sarah into a slim navy skirt, matching jacket and a plain white blouse, the *amah* braiding her hair, letting it hang down her back. A small hat, held on by hatpins, finished her toilet, Mei-mei giggling beside her, who was fumbling in her elaborate knot of hair on the top of her head, to produce a small stiletto.

Sarah gaped, as the little *amah* returned it to its hiding place. "You plenty safe," patting her hair, confidently.

"Thank you, I'm comforted," was all Sarah could murmur. This was fast becoming a Drury Lane farce.

Simon rose to his feet as she re-entered the room, his quick nod at her outfit assured her that he approved. "I see you have come prepared," with a wicked glance at her hat, which brought a martial stare to her cold eyes.

"How else do you think I could keep a hat on my head?" she snapped.

He turned to Mrs. Merton, who was

looking a trifle perplexed, at Sarah's curt tone.

"I promise, Daphne, to be on my best behaviour and don't worry, we're only sparring with each other," with a bow to Sarah, who was seething at his audacity, not a little perturbed at the prospect of an afternoon spent in his company.

Couldn't Aunt Daphne sense what a arrogant rogue he was? Oh, why hadn't she told her about his outrageous offer for then she would not have been in this pickle.

Sarah bid Aunt Daphne goodbye, before sweeping past her tormentor, as regal as any duchess, through the hall and on to the pavement, where his carriage awaited.

"I sincerely feel for you, Miss Sarah," he murmured, unrepentant. "I promise you a wonderful afternoon," his usual aloof air missing.

"I hope I'm seasick!" was all she found to retort, lowering her eyes as he handed her into the carriage.

"Your *amah* will deal with that," optimistically, ordering the groom to let go the horses.

"Oh!" she fumed. "It would have served you right, if I had told Aunt Daphne what a rogue you are."

"Come, it's a beautiful afternoon," he coaxed, with a smile which had been the undoing of many an unwary competitor. "I did promise to see that no harm would come to you, word of a gentleman," with a quick glance at her.

They drove around the bay at a spanking pace, Sarah still too upset to admire his skill with the ribbons, but did notice how men kowtowed to him as they passed.

An uneasy silence fell between them, until Simon said, "I have asked you to come sailing with me, Miss Sarah, because I'm truly repentant for my very improper proposal. If I had known, or sensed that it would have been so obnoxious to you, I would have refrained," meeting her astonished

269

stare, his smile rueful. "I would really like you to experience the exhilaration one feels, when sailing a clipper and I'm hopeful to see those cold eyes, forgive. I must add, that I still think you are the most challenging young lady I've met for some time."

"I'd like to remind you that we're barely acquainted," fighting to retain her dignity.

"I could always remedy that," came the swift reply and when she turned away added, "Let's forget my *faux pas*; I made a mistake," leaving her with no quick retort.

He helped the girls into a small boat and were rowed out to the ship and soon on board. Certain orders were given, the sails catching the brisk breeze, Sarah hanging on to the rail and soon they were out into the ocean. The clipper had taken flight on the wings of the wind.

From then on, she had no fault to find in Mr. Mac Gowan's manner towards her, his worldly *savoir faire* making him an agreeable host. It was a perfect afternoon and an exhilarating one for Sarah, so different from a large ocean liner and soon found her body at one with the swift changes of the ship, but was still a little distant, Simon appearing not to notice, as he kept her entertained, to ask her if she would like to control his ship, but first, she must watch what he did, leading her to a bench close by, while he took the wheel.

He must be in his late thirties, she judged, his fair hair liberally sprinkled with silver. It was very evident that he was doing something that he revelled in, being in complete control of his huge ship, playing her like a master, which he was.

He caught her assessing glance, to smile across at her, handing the wheel over to the helmsman, for a moment. "Now come, Miss Sarah," taking her by the arm. "I'll teach you to sail, so that you too, may experience the thrill of feeling a live ship under your control," and proceeded to give her a lesson, standing close behind her, ready to grab the wheel if necessary, but as he felt the stiffening of her young body, he drew back.

"You're sailing my clipper," he shouted.

She could only nod, her face a happy glow.

"I'm not really content or completely satisfied, unless I'm sailing. It's in the blood. My Scottish ancestors were reivers," and she could well believe that, quite at ease now with the *tai-pan*, thrilling at the sweep of the boat, Simon nodding, satisfied.

In her pleasure, Sarah forgot to be distant, Simon smiling to himself. What a companion she would make and regret filled him. He would dearly like to sail the seven seas with her.

With a smile he handed the wheel back again to the helmsman, leading her down into the main cabin, Mei-mei close on their heels, Sarah holding back a chuckle.

"It's incredibly cosy," was her only comment, as she and the *amah* were shown into a well-appointed Powder Room, that had been especially furnished to please a lady, Sarah raising an eyebrow, Mei-mei for once silenced, her black eyes as round as saucers.

Back on deck Simon was waiting, leading the way to several chairs under an awning, where tea was being served, with crunchy biscuits made from coarsely ground almonds and honey, which she ravenously ate. The sea must have made her hungry.

Simon glanced across at her, imaging her in breeches and a silk shirt, the wind etching every line of her slim body, that glorious hair loose. Why had his assessment of her been so faulty, was it because she had to work for a living?

Sarah quickly sensed the change in him, cynicism had no place in this heavenly afternoon and caught a glimpse of what he must have been like as a young man, before he had become a hardened *tai-pan*.

He was the first to break the companionable silence, to say softly, "Miss Sarah, you're the thermals under my wings."

She had trouble in containing her amusement, but it still spilled over in her smile and dancing eyes. "No, no!" she protested, seeing the angry movement of his hands and the tightening of his mouth, "That was beautiful! Nobody has ever said that to me before."

"I meant it as a compliment," he said stiffly.

"But — but, I'm not used to such high-falutin' phrases. Your years in the Orient must have rubbed off on you."

"It came out very naturally," he said, still a little on his dignity. "I've lived with the wind all my life. It has filled my sails and have learned to heed it, for it is no respecter of persons. It has filled my pockets."

"But what do you do when a typhoon strikes? I have heard so much about these winds since I've been here and the havoc they cause."

"*Tai-fung*, Supreme Winds! Sailors know when one is brewing and one makes all haste for the nearest safe harbour and simply ride it out, hoping for the best, accepting one's *joss* — one's fate," he explained. "They swoop out of the China Seas and are terrifying," his voice sombre. "One can lose millions if your ships are sunk."

He turned to her with a smile. "You appear to be very interested, Miss Sarah. Are you regretting having turned down my offer," some of his old cynicism back. She hurriedly denied this. "I was merely making polite conversation, otherwise horrible silences fall."

He chuckled, his good humour restored. "Have you a family, may I ask and who is your father?"

"All I can say is, had I accepted your offer, it would have gone against all the tenets of what is expected of me."

"Ah, then your birth is good?"

"My parents died years ago and I live with my brother — "

"And who is your brother, may I ask? It is most unusual for a girl of your quality to have to seek employment and I think I may be forgiven for offering you *carte blanche*," a remark which she chose to ignore.

"I have never been able to get on with my sister-in-law and nursing is my only option. At least it is now a recognized profession, thanks to Florence Nightingale."

"You could marry — " quizzing her.

"I'd have to be asked first," she reminded him, with a smile.

"True, but I should think you'll have no problem there. Who is your brother, by the way?" he asked again, becoming a little bored by this conversation. Not once had she been even vaguely aware of him as a man. It was a novel experience, which he did not particularly care for, his self-esteem slightly dented.

"If you really would like to know," noticing his disinterest, "he's in Government and was, at one time, in the Ministry of Exports and Imports."

He sat up suddenly. "By Jove! I know Bertram Danbury, to my cost," his tone rueful. "He's a stickler for the truth," taking a pinch of snuff, Sarah, naughtily thinking that in the years to come, the *tai-pan* would have a yellow nose.

"And your father?" he asked curiously.

"My grandfather was Lord Chadton."

He opened his eyes wide. "Was he indeed! And your father?" he insisted.

"He was a second son and when my parents died, Bertram took me into his household," her voice deadened to such an extent, that he was able to get a very good idea of what her home life must have been like.

"Was that why you took the position of Daphne's companion?" He had begun to understand. "*Meâ culpâ!*" sincerely contrite. "Forgive me. I had no right to treat you as I did."

She accepted his apology, lowering her gaze, but not quick enough to hide a momentarily flash of anger, despising him for his double standards.

She had a temper, it could not be otherwise, with that tawny head of hers and those emerald eyes. It must have taken a lot of courage to do what she had done, he thought with admiration.

Sarah went on to tell him how she had visited the hospital and would be allowed to join the nursing staff, on her return.

He was sitting back, watching her lazily. "I could easily sail away with you — "

"But you won't," she replied confidently, "because of whom my grandfather was," her eyes steady, challenging.

He shouted with laughter, extending a careless finger to flick the cheek nearest to him. "I like you, Sarah Danbury," but deep down anger at himself was being born, upset that he had made such a gross error in his opinion of her. She would have made him an excellent wife and a mother for his heir, he thought with regret.

He took her hand and lightly kissed her fingers. "My thanks, Miss Sarah, for a very pleasant afternoon. Come, we are now entering the harbour," and as they waited for the skiff to fetch them, he pointed out HMS Vengeance that had just arrived, swaying gently with the swell of the tide.

Sarah sighed. "I've had the most lovely afternoon, thank you, *Tai-Pan*."

"The pleasure was all mine, we'll soon make a sailor of you. The wind and the sun has given you a lovely colour," pleased that she had reverted back to using his title.

They landed at the wharf, Simon's groom already there with the carriage and Simon was helping Sarah into it, when a sedan-chair drew to a halt. In it was Sophia Nedling. Surely this beautiful woman must have Irish ancestry, thought Sarah, that black hair, those deep blue eyes, spoke of that. She was wearing a gown similar to ones Sarah had seen in a women's magazine, just before she had left London and a head-hugging cap of flowers. She must have just come from a late afternoon function.

"Simon," she called, leaning out of the window, smiling at him in the most provocative way. "I do hope you are remembering we are to dine with Emily Hornton and attend her soirée this evening?" she said, playfully tapping his arm with her fan. "Mind that you are there, for you are the most entertaining of all my escorts that this god-forsaken island can offer."

Simon's reply was coolly polite. "If I'm not there, Sophia, you'll find someone else to squire you. It should be easy enough," looking down his high-bridged nose.

"Of course I know that," she retorted, her dimples appearing, "but I'd much rather have you, *Tai-Pan*." With that she withdrew her head, giving the

280

bearers an order to proceed.

It was dusk as Sarah and Simon drove around the bay, a fairyland scene. All the lamps on the ships were twinkling like so many stars, Sarah suddenly silent, common sense returning. How could she have been so friendly with this man. He'd get ideas, if he hadn't them already, betraying her agitation.

Simon was distinctly quizzical, appreciative of her dilemma. "I also enjoyed this afternoon as much as you did. Will you come with me to the races?"

"I don't think I'll have the chance," she replied matter-of-factly. "I don't yet know when Mr. Merton will be booking my passage home."

Simon very well aware of her returned wariness, kept silent. He would bide his time, but was brought down to earth by her,

"Why did you invite me to go sailing with you, Mr. Mac Gowan?" in a no nonsense voice.

His reply was prompt. "I enjoy your company, as I've said before."

They arrived at the Merton's residence, Simon helping Sarah down, accompanying her to the door, to find Daphne in the hall, Mr. Briggs muttering in the background.

It had been an uncomfortable afternoon for her, a little afraid that she had been too persistent in making Sarah accept Simon's invitation. The child had been almost loathe to accept, but one look at her calm face, put her fears to rest.

"I was becoming a little anxious about you both," she confessed. "It is rather late."

Simon was contrite. "Forgive me, Daphne, for causing you distress, but it was real sailing weather," with a bow, refusing her offer of refreshment, saying that he would see them both again, at Mrs. Summerfield's musical evening on the morrow. "Miss Danbury, your servant," with another bow, his usually cold eyes twinkling audaciously, before leaving with a jaunty stride.

Aunt Daphne, naturally wanted to know all about her jaunt, ordering tea, as they passed into the drawing room. "You realise, of course, that Simon's clippers and his name are a byword here in the East?"

"It was a perfect afternoon," replied Sarah happily. "To sail in that beautiful ship, adorned in all her glory, is something I'll not forget. I felt free from any earth bond," pausing as Mei-mei brought in the teatray.

"Much talky, talky, *tai-pan*," she grinned, arranging small tables in front of the ladies.

"Perhaps you don't realize, dear, but you have been highly honoured. I have never heard of Simon inviting any other young lady to share an afternoon of sailing with him. Oh my! Sarah my dear," she enthused. "What a feather in your cap if he were to propose to you," going into ecstasies at the very thought, to add, waspishly "And one in the eye for that awful Sophia Nedling!"

"Aunt Daphne, I think there is something you should know," trying to smile, but it was a woeful attempt.

When she heard about Simon's improper proposal, she was livid. "Oh, my poor dear! I remember that you were unwilling to accept his invitation. Please forgive me!" shocked. "Did he — and why did you not tell me?"

Sarah assured her that she had not suffered any more insults and that in fact, Mr. Mac Gowan had been an excellent host, his behaviour exemplary. "I really did enjoy sailing in that beautiful clipper and felt as free as she was. I just can't explain it."

However, Aunt Daphne was still shocked, "And I want to know how he found out that you were in my employ," she snapped. "It could only have been that gabble-bag, Mattie. I did tell her, before I left for Britain, that I would need help on the voyage. Well! I certainly will have something to say to that Madam, when next I see her."

"Aunt Daphne, I think it was Miss Nedling, who told Mr. Mac Gowan, because she whispered something to him, when he and I were at the flower market."

"That woman!" she exploded again.

"I would like to suggest that you don't change your attitude towards Mr. Mac Gowan. This would really set people talking and I wouldn't want that."

"But, but he — he was despicable!" she spluttered. "He won't bother me again," adding with a gurgle. "He found out that I come from a very good family, telling him that my grandfather was Lord Chadton. Aunt Daphne, you should have seen his disconcerted face!" with another chuckle. "And you, dear Aunt, look like a pouter-pigeon."

"I can well believe it," she said indignantly, but with a quiver. "Very well," she agreed, though reluctantly. "This will go no further and I admire your fortitude," and began to laugh. "What a shock to the *tai-pan*'s ego.

Well done, but pouter-pigeon?" raising an eyebrow.

Sarah nodded with an impish grin. "But is that all you can say, about this matter?"

"My dear, you must surely know that men keep mistresses," she said comfortably, but could not forgive, or excuse Simon for not recognising this girl's quality.

Meanwhile, Simon was driving furiously to his office, a grimace of self-mockery, making his face even more austere. He had never been caught so wrong-footed before. "Damn it!" his usual *éclat* missing. "You bungling ass! Couldn't you have seen, felt, that she was gently born?" throwing the reins at his groom, telling him to go home and stormed into his emporium, banging the doors behind him. However, he quickly regained his equilibrium, wondering if Sarah would accept a proposal of marriage from him. It would be better than taking up nursing. His spirits rose.

Later that afternoon, when Mr. Merton returned home, his wife heard that men were betting at the club as to the outcome of the friendship between Simon Mac Gowan and Miss Danbury.

"How utterly beastly of them!" came her hot rejoinder.

6

AT breakfast the following morning, Aunt Daphne announced that they were to attend an official afternoon, at the governor's residence. "William has made an appointment for us. It is usual for new-comers to our colony, to pay a courtesy call on him, so please wear your prettiest afternoon frock. I would like to suggest your sea green one and, of course, a hat."

As they were being driven to the governor's residence, Aunt Daphne began talking about Sir Arthur Kennedy. "He came to us in early '72, his background army and governorships in several British lands. Unfortunately, he lost his dear wife some time ago. Lady Kennedy was greatly revered by us all, a gentle, gracious lady and is sorely missed. Some say he is a harsh man, because he brought in branding and deportation, but crime has to be fought," wagging a finger, "for how, otherwise, can law abiding citizens live in safety?"

Aunt Daphne and Sarah were shown into a side room, that had been set apart for the ladies' wraps and where they could spruce up, Aunt Daphne casting a critical eye over her protégé, approving the style that was cut high under the bosom to fall in graceful folds to her gold slippered feet, her small straw bonnet tied with the same coloured ribbons, meeting Sarah's amused eyes.

The afternoon went well, the governor welcoming Sarah with a kindly smile, saying that he hoped her stay in the colony would be of some duration, before moving away to speak to another guest. A very informal afternoon, a lot of the guests Sarah had already met. It was another snippet of news for Priscilla when next she wrote to her family.

On the way home, Aunt Daphne

mentioned that she was thinking of holding another party soon, Sarah again, offering to write out the invitations.

"Please, dear, remember to send one to Dick and to Mr. Carew. Perhaps, he'll be able to attend this time. I haven't even met him yet," accepting Mr. Briggs' hand, as she stepped out of the carriage to bustle inside.

Several mornings later, at breakfast, which consisted of fish, rice and tea or ale, Mr. Merton also remembered the two men and was assured that both had been sent invitations, that led Aunt Daphne to enquire if he had had any news of Agnes. "That young woman has me worried!"

He nodded. "We have found out that she is staying with Mr. Timms' brother and sister-in-law and is not yet engaged or married, but we have no idea yet, if she will be willing to catch the next boat. Our courier found her very undecided. However, a berth has been booked for her."

His wife sank back into her chair,

with a sigh. "What a dreadful mix-up! Have you told Dick all this?"

"How could I? What if Agnes does not arrive, but I have told that young man that he must meet the next liner. I'm hoping that the child will have enough gumption and decide to arrive." He grinned, looking a great deal younger. "Heaven help me if I ever have to play cupid again!" he said with strong feeling.

"Agnes should have been told how much that poor boy is suffering," with a worried frown.

"That poor boy is twenty-four years old and what if Agnes changes her mind again? We've done our best, but far better he doesn't know."

Aunt Daphne nodded, her husband excusing himself from the table. "I must rush off, dear. Hopefully, I'll be able to come home in time for your party," kissing her scented cheek.

Dick arrived early, very aware of Sarah every time she entered the room, giving her soulful glances, Sarah getting him to help Mr. Briggs with the drinks tables.

Guests began to arrive, Sarah seeing that they all found seats, the band playing softly, barely heard above the hum of voices.

Hector Carew arrived, but as chance had it, Mr. Briggs was absent from his post to welcome him. He was a tall, well-built young man, with deep blue eyes and dark hair, turning a little impatiently as a lady entered the hall.

Sarah moved forward quickly to welcome the guest, noticing the butler's absence, her hand held out, but stopped short, staring at him, with a smile that lit her features, accompanied by a breathlessness that left her gasping, with surprise and joy.

"Hector Carew, Ma'am," his voice pleasantly pitched.

The gentleman who had just arrived was her Stranger, a surge of happiness racing through her, the silver sheen of joyous tears sparkling her eyes, Mr. Carew thinking what a young, vibrant little creature this was, smiling down at her, smiling at her exuberant greeting. Was she the daughter of the house, he wondered idly.

Sarah's smile faded as quickly as it had been born. No recollection burst from his steady glance and she turned away, hiding her hurt, her face changing to one of sadness, catching back a sob. For a moment she held her breath. Would he remember her, but no, there was only a rueful smile troubling his sensitive mouth, as he asked her if she was all right, in a deep voice that she remembered so well.

She nodded mutely, her pulses throbbing uncomfortably, having a strong impulse to blurt out who she was, but it would not do. Several other guests had arrived who had witnessed this meeting, a little surprised at Sarah's swift withdrawal and began to speculate as to why Miss Danbury should be welcoming Daphne's guests. Where was Mr. Briggs?

Sarah quickly gathered her wits,

thankful that her unruly tongue had not betrayed her. "Thank you, Sir. It must be the heat. I'm newly come from Britain," she said over brightly.

Mr. Briggs hurried into the room, begging the guests pardon and Sarah heard Mr. Carew say, that he urgently needed to see Mr. Merton, who fortunately, at that moment came into the hall, Mr. Carew turning to him in relief.

"Sir, just as I was about to leave the office, a naval officer arrived with a package for you. One of our warships has just docked. I thought you should know, Sir."

"Good lad!" his expression grave. "We'll both go back," and turned to Sarah to ask her to make his apologies to his wife and he hoped they both would soon return.

She nodded, but all she could think of was that her Stranger had not recognised her, while Mr. Carew accompanying his superior to the office, wondered why that friendly girl's happy expression had suddenly been doused like a candle, then forgot her, as they were driven to the government buildings.

Sarah sought out Aunt Daphne and gave her the message, Aunt Daphne glancing quickly at her white face, hurrying her into the cloak-room and rang for tea, a panacea for all ills, as far as she was concerned. "I can do with a moment's peace, myself, but dear, what made you look so washed out? Sit down," thrusting a vinaigrette under her nose. "It is quite a squeeze in there. Most gratifying, I must say!"

Sarah pulled herself together, giving her benefactress a wavering smile, longing to tell her what had happened and the heartache.

Aunt Daphne gave her a loving pat. "I know, you've rushed around too much today, my dear and I do appreciate it. Bless you!"

It was much later when the two gentlemen returned and by that time, Sarah had herself well in hand as Mr.

Merton introduced the gentleman to her and Aunt Daphne, who welcomed him into their midst, Mr. Carew saying to Sarah, that he was pleased to see that she had regained her colour, begging pardon that he had had to rush away like that. She smiled at him, saying that it had been a hectic day.

"I'd like to share this waltz with you, Miss Danbury, if I may?" placing an arm around her waist, to swing her into the dance.

The hand holding hers was large and quite impersonal. That kiss, those loving words had been nothing but a charade, meaning nothing, she reflected sadly, none of these thoughts reflected in her expression, which she fought to keep cheerful. The dance came to an end, Sarah thankful to be seated next to Aunt Daphne again, Mr. Carew to join the gentlemen in the card room, smiling as he remembered his first sight of Miss Danbury, stepping out of her petticoat, looking around to find that

Mr. Mac Gowan was not amongst the guests.

The lady who was sitting on the other side of Sarah and who had witnessed her meeting with Mr. Carew, whispered, "Don't get any romantic ideas in that direction, dear," she tittered. "He keeps very much to himself. Probably an old love frosted, but very pleasant and gentlemanly. I met him at Lady Philpot's musical evening. Single men, of course, are much sought after here in the colony. You'll be returning home soon?" she enquired sweetly.

Sarah nodded coolly. "Yes, I have to get back. I'm to join Florence Nightingale's nurses," which effectively, silenced that lady.

Further down the row were seated two spinsters, who had also witnessed this little drama. Jane and Esmerelda Finch.

"A new face amongst us, Jane. How nice and such a charming young man, too. I wonder what made Miss Sarah go all faint, hmm?" inquisitively. "I peeped into the hall on my way to the powder room and saw her go pale at the sight of him."

"It was the heat and don't get any silly romantic notions about them. Mr. Carew is only here on a temporary basis, Esmerelda," she warned severely.

"Oh, yes, from the Calcutta office, so I've heard though I can't help but compare his very natty mode of dress, with that of Dick Forbes' rather casual one."

Sarah again danced with Mr. Carew, Dick hovering in the background, barely able to conceal his jealousy, that made her partner comment,

"That young man is top over tail in love with you. If looks could kill, I'd be six feet under."

"Dick?" her surprise causing him to smile. "He's just dreadfully lonely and hurt. Surely you must know about Agnes?" and when he nodded added, "I don't think it is generally known that Mr. Merton has been making enquiries about Agnes and has hopes that she might still rejoin Dick."

"I know my superior is kindly, but what can he do?"

"Evidently, she isn't married yet and could change her mind. I hope so."

Mr. Carew looked doubtful, keeping his thoughts to himself, asking about London.

"It's still very much the same," she replied, "but I'm happy to be missing the winter."

He swung her around again to say gloomily, "I've had no letters from home for months. Some ass in the Calcutta office must have crammed them into a drawer and forgotten about them."

"I have heard that several P & O ships have been lost because of storms. Thank goodness, we didn't have to face one, although the Bay of Biscay was pretty awful," she disclosed, thinking of poor Aunt Daphne. "Perhaps your mail will turn up soon and items do go astray. I haven't had a reply yet from my family to letters I wrote and posted en route."

Dick claimed the last dance, grousing that he hadn't had much chance to chat to her. "I miss Agnes dreadfully," he mourned. "Before she sailed, I wrote every night to her, but now — " Sarah dearly wishing that she could give him some hope.

Late that evening, or was it early morning, she sank tiredly, into her bed, utterly drained of all emotion. Her dreams of meeting her Stranger had come about, but not for a moment had she ever imagined that he would not recognise her. She had travelled half across the world to miraculously find him. Hector Carew, savouring his name, on a hiccough, deciding that it suited him, but — at last she allowed her heartache to spill over. That night, her pillow was wet with tears.

The following morning, Sarah woke very early, her sleep having been extremely disturbed, Mr. Carew flitting through her dreams to an uncomfortable degree. Had that sweet interlude at her betrothal party, she wondered again, been merely an amusing trifle of the moment, but deep inside, she found this distasteful. One thing she was sure of, that there had been no recognition in his eyes, no surprise in his manner.

From this, she regained her confidence, holding her face in her hands, to hide the happy smile, even from herself, cuddling down again into her pillows. Perhaps, they could become friends and on this positive thought, fell into a peaceful sleep.

At the breakfast table, Aunt Daphne, naturally, discussed her party, saying how delighted she was that Sarah had been accepted by the community, chuckling, "And I'm sure the *tai-pan* is not going to tittle tattle. Some of my friends though, think that you are more than a little eccentric, to have a wish to join Mrs. Florence Nightingale's nursing staff, although Edna did hasten to add, that nobody would dare call that lady eccentric."

"But I thought she was single," Sarah surprised.

"Oh, yes, it's an honorary title bestowed on her," to say with a beam. "I never thought, when you came to my aid, that I would have so much pleasure and help from you. My dear, I'm determined that you shall win the heart of some eligible gentleman, not Simon," she firmly decided.

Sarah thought it time to change the subject. "Aunt Daphne, may I have Mei-mei for a few hours? I wish to purchase another evening gown and Mei-mei knows of a dress shop," consent was graciously given. "Also dear Aunt, I really should think of going back home. I can't presume on your hospitality much longer and how kind you have been to me," smiling fondly at her.

"Well, at least stay for the Governor's Ball," she coaxed, to which Sarah happily agreed.

The small Chinese shop, to which Mei-mei took her, was tucked in between two large buildings, no window for display, but the little *amah* confidently, led the way into the interior, where rows of rails held gowns of every hue and style, even catering for high-born Chinese ladies.

Eventually they found a gown fashioned in georgette, cut high-waisted, with tiny puffed sleeves, which caught the girls' fancy. It was in a delicate shade of honey, that suited Sarah's colouring and when she tried it on, fitted her to perfection and what was more, the price was right.

The old, wizened little man rummaged around to find paper in which to wrap it and bowed to the two satisfied customers as they left. Did the Chinese never smile?

They passed through a short street where a lot of men were playing Mah Jong on the pavement, the rattle of ivory tiles, Sarah likening to the chirping of myriads of small birds, the tiles beautifully painted and when she asked Mr. Merton about them later, was told that the game was similar to rummy. As they turned into another alleyway, they suddenly came on a man, cruelly thrashing his dog and Sarah saw red, flying to the animal's defence.

"No talky talky that man," pleaded Mei-mei, trying to hold her back. "Not good, not good, Missie!"

Hector had, on that particular morning, been asked by his chief to deliver an important document to their lawyers and was feeling decidedly disgruntled. Seriously reviewing his whole career, he wondered if his roving days were over. Should he ask for a transfer back to the London office and settle down? All the travelling he had done, was beginning to pall. His feelings of uncertainty, however, vanished when to his surprise, he caught sight of Miss Danbury, having a fierce argument with a burley dock worker. He shouted to the chairmen to stop, paid them off and hurriedly lengthened his stride, fearful for her safety. He knew men of the East did not tolerate interference from females. Already a small crowd had gathered, some supportive, others in the majority.

Sarah was trying to thrust money into the man's hand, her greeny eyes ablaze. "Don't you dare hit that dog again. He's one of God's creatures!"

There was no expression on the man's face, except his glance, that showed his contempt, as he threw down the rope and stalked off.

"May I see you home, Miss Danbury?" Hector asked quietly, applauding her spirited attack and stormy eyes that still sparked fire.

"No thank you, Mr. Carew," conscious of him for the first time, her glance still on the animal, who was madly wagging his whole body. "You are free to go, my friend," giving him a gentle pat.

"Watch him run for his life — " began Hector.

"He's free to do what he will," but the animal refused to budge, gazing soulfully up into her face, his tail still wagging. "I'll take him home, Mr. Carew."

"He's extremely dirty — "

"Yes, I'll bath and feed him," looking down at the animal again, a little doubtfully. What had she done?

"He's your friend for life. Come," cupping her elbow. "He'll follow us. What are you going to do with the brute?" he asked as they walked along to a rickshaw rank.

"I don't know yet," she replied candidly.

"You were very intrepid, Miss Danbury," he murmured admiringly. "Well done, but it could have turned nasty."

"You mean that I did not act as a nicely brought up young lady should?" her chin in the air, challenging him.

A chuckle broke from him, which he turned quickly into a cough.

"Do you think I should not have interfered?" she asked militantly.

"No, no, it is what I would have

done myself, but will Mrs. Merton be pleased?"

"She won't mind," hopefully, "Her son, Harry is always bringing strays home," she confided airily. "And I'm going to call him Hong?" this on the spur of the moment.

Hector again hid his amusement. This was a misnomer, if there ever was one. Hong meant fragrant, but kept this small detail to himself, well aware that she would retort that after the dog had been bathed and trimmed, he would be just that.

He handed Sarah and Mei-mei into a rickshaw, Sarah holding out her hand in a friendly fashion, a grin breaking through. "Thank you, Mr. Carew," she said demurely.

"But I didn't do a thing," he protested quickly.

"You were there," she replied simply.

He stepped back, touching his hat, watching the rickshaw until it was out of sight, with amused approval.

It was Sunday again and this time Mr. Merton had invited both Dick and Hector to lunch and to spend the afternoon with the family, Mr. Merton saying that it wasn't any fun to be stuck in hotel suites, Dick again particularly pleased by this invitation. He had attended every function that Sarah had attended, but she was becoming a little bored by him. Benevolence could be a little overdone, she found. Both gentlemen arrived, Hector commenting on Hong's appearance, saying he wouldn't have recognized the animal, Sarah replying that he had become great friends with Mr. Briggs, accompanying him on his market forays no end, "Unless Mei-mei or I need him for a body guard, of course," with her friendly smile.

After Church and a light luncheon, they all piled into Mr. Merton's spacious open carriage, Sarah sitting next to Hector, that drew dark looks from Dick, sitting opposite, until their host whispered an admonition, Dick sinking deeper into the seat with a mutter.

"Please, may Agnes be on that ship this week," prayed Mr. Merton fervently. He had had enough of this young pup.

As they drove off, he asked Hector what he most would like to see. "Sir, I believe there is a yacht race, this afternoon should see their return."

A lot of other folk were like minded and the promenade was alive with chattering people, the betting heavy.

The first yacht sailed in soon after, the others following close behind, allowing the little party to walk back to their carriage, Dick taking Sarah's arm possessively, murmuring, "Miss Sarah, your eyebrows are like a pair of swallows' wings. You're beautiful!"

Sarah trying hard to refrain from giggling, could only reply in a stifled voice, "But — but they're not black, but ginger," she corrected with a twinkle.

"Oh, you know what I mean!" smiling down at her shyly. "I'm not really a lady's man. I — I love Agnes," with a gulp.

"Yes, I know," she soothed, "and I do hope, most sincerely, for a happy outcome," longing to tell him that his lady love would be on the next boat.

The carriage moved off, Dick seated next to Sarah, much to his satisfaction, throwing Hector a smug smirk. They passed a beautiful Chinese temple, Harry saying, "And you like the way the four corners of the roof tip their ends to the heavens, Sarah, don't you?"

"The Chinese architecture is beautiful," conceded Hector, "but what has impressed me most, is the size of Hong Kong and all its development. After all, it is only thirty-four years, or so, since it has become a crown colony."

"British expertise, my boy," said Mr. Merton simply.

"Queen Victoria and her Foreign Secretary, Lord Palmerston were not too happy at the annexing," piped up Harry again. "But Hong Kong now is a trading centre, also a port for careening and refilling our ships."

Both his parents looked at him in amazement, his father saying, "My dear lad, I've been underestimating you, quite dreadfully!"

"Papa," he replied indignantly, "That's our history and if we don't do well, the headmistress, Miss Finch, has lots to say about that!"

"Both Finch sisters teach in our British School," explained Mrs. Merton, "and what hard working women they are, too. Hector, we're fortunate in having their services," who replied in a conversational way, having also done his homework, before leaving Calcutta, "This country also has a history of politics, scandal broth, opium and gunboat diplomacy, plus the fact, it has the safest sea port in the Far East."

"Not forgetting the lucrative tea trade. If it were not for tea, we would have to use brandy or whiskey to make our water safe to drink," reminded Mr. Merton.

The following evening at dinner, Mr. Merton, very pleased with himself, suggested that they all meet the P & O liner that was due in on the morrow.

His wife turned to him. "Oh, William, is Agnes to be on the boat, do you know? I do hope so," she breathed fervently and when he nodded, "This is your doing, I think, my dear."

He nodded. "I have great hopes. We gave her an ultimatum, that if she did not avail herself of this opportunity, then the offer would be withdrawn for all time. Perhaps, a little harsh, but perhaps she needed that jolt."

"Have you told Dick," she asked, with a happy glance at Sarah, who was equally pleased.

"I've given that young man, who by the way, I'm heartily sick of, strict instructions to meet the boat, but he's under the impression, that he'll be meeting a colleague, arriving back from furlough," and for a brief moment, there was something like an impish grin that broke from him.

"We'll certainly be there," promised Aunt Daphne, rising from the table, to give orders to the staff to arrange an early breakfast.

The usual people were on the wharf the following morning, folk looking out eagerly for familiar faces, or inquisitively, scanning the list of arrivals and by the time the Merton household had arrived, the first passengers were already coming ashore.

The family greeted Dick, who had not appreciated having to get up so early. "Mr. Merton, Sir, who am I supposed to meet? You quite forgot to give me the gentleman's name," with a worried frown.

It was Sarah who spotted Agnes first and nudged Mr. Merton, pointing as she did so. Dick noticed and looked up. For a moment he was silent, not believing his eyes and then with a whoop, "Agnes!" and began pushing against the descending crowd, with all their hand luggage, shouting and waving his arms, until he reached his love and grabbed her.

A great cheer went up from the spectators, Hector, who had arrived too, murmuring to Sarah, "I'm glad that he's got his heart desire," with a twisted smile.

She nodded, with a wide smile and wished for the hundredth time that he would recognise her.

"I wish them all the happiness in the world," said Aunt Daphne, dabbing her eyes with a wisp of lace.

"Amen!" said Harry, under his breath to Sarah, with a naughty glance. "Hope you won't miss Dick too much, Sarah?"

"That's enough from you, saucebox," she retaliated, as they followed Mr. Merton to the carriage, who was saying to his spouse that the office wouldn't be seeing Dick for the rest of the day.

Several days later, Agnes' story began to be made known. She had stayed with Mr. Timms' relatives, but after the courier had left, matters came to a head, Mr. Timms deciding that he didn't think it was the right time for him to be thinking of marriage. Agnes then upped and sought sanctuary with the Bishop's family.

The community accepted her story, praising and complimenting her on her resourcefulness in a trying situation, Dick proud of her.

Aunt Daphne was amazed and pleased. "I wouldn't have thought she had that much sense in her. I'm impressed and I've heard that the Gilberts have taken her in, until the marriage. I do like happy endings," Sarah agreeing.

The next event was a prestigious one, a charity ball organised by the ladies to raise funds for destitute children and for the campaign to stop the binding of children's feet in the colony. This yearly event was always held at the residence of Mr. Mac Gowan, but the cost of the tickets, thought Sarah, was astronomically high, Aunt Daphne agreeing, "but it is for two very good causes and you'll see, everyone will accept," she said confidently.

Sarah had again offered her services, Aunt Daphne adamant that she was also invited and wrote her name on the list, with a tick against it.

Sarah smiled as she sat down to her task. She would, after all, be able to see the *tai-pan*'s home of which she had heard so much.

The eagerly awaited evening arrived, Mei-mei brushing Sarah's hair to the mandatory hundred strokes and then helped her dress, buttoning up the thirty or more tiny pearl buttons, before tying her curls back with a simple bow and a string of dainty incandescent shells, her only ornament, these having been bought at one of the stalls.

The *amah* stood back, with a satisfied nod. "Plenty men talky talky you tonight," she said with a grin, Sarah thanking her for her help.

Harry also grinned at her as she came

downstairs, saying that she looked bang up to the nines, Sarah replying that that was a compliment indeed coming from him, but it was left to Mr. Merton to say that she would be the belle of the ball, his glance admiring her gown of honey georgette, that she had purchased from the elderly Chinese and that of his wife's, who was regal in a royal blue taffeta, which suited her fuller figure admirably, with diamonds at her throat. "You both look magnificent," Sarah smiling her thanks, picking up her shawl.

"Your carriage is at the door, Sir," announced Mr. Briggs, shepherding the small group to the carriage, wishing them a pleasant evening, Harry waving to them as they drove away.

As they passed under the street lights, Mr. Merton murmured to Sarah, his glance going to her shining gold red hair. "Don't break too many hearts tonight, my dear, amongst them the younger members of my staff. They have to work tomorrow remember, also those amongst my older personnel," he added *sotto voce*.

Aunt Daphne sank back against the comfortable squabs to say, "Now, Sarah dear, I shall tell you what to expect when we enter the *tai-pan*'s home, to save you from gauping. First of all, there are a great many priceless china and porcelain items and other fancy nicknacks in every room, all priceless and not to my taste, but very valuable for all that," her husband keeping a smile to himself, at her phrasing. She was an endearing joy to him, listening lazily to what she was saying. "The ball room is as ornate as any you will see at home, lavishly decorated, but with flowers which the *tai-pan* would have ordered from Nanking."

The carriage was slowing down, Mr. Merton leaning forward to point out the huge, sprawling house, that could be faintly seen on the hillside, as the road wound up higher and higher, Sarah noting that there were very few other houses dotting the area.

"But — but, it looks so very similar to all the other properties, functional," she said with keen disappointment. "Douglas Castle, over there," with a wave of her hand, "is far more impressive."

"Wait until you see inside," promised Aunt Daphne.

The coachman stopped at ornate gates, to be waved on by a lackey, brandishing a lantern and then on up, to stop, two servants springing forward to open the carriage doors, helping them to alight, on to a wide expanse of red carpeting, stretching to the ornate entrance, the area brightly lit, to be ushered into a large, lofty hall, twin staircases rising from it in graceful curves, to meet in the centre of the gallery, that ran along three sides of the room.

Sarah could only stand and stare, oblivious to the other guests around her.

"Wait until you see the ballroom," murmured Aunt Daphne, prodding her in the back, to join the queue, where Mrs. Thomson, one of the committee members was welcoming guests, before waving them on.

All this — this ostentation must surely resemble a palace of some Eastern potentate, Sarah's thoughts fleeting and without envy, as they walked through several rooms, to admire jade vases in profusion, articles of Chinese and Indian art, fat Buddhas, staring down benignly at one. It was all too much. Who did the dusting?

"One wonders if the *tai-pan*'s personal suite, is this cluttered?" Aunt Daphne asked, with some exasperation. "Possessions are ruling this man's life."

Sarah suppressed a chuckle. "I can't ever really imagine being mistress of this kind of house, oh, I forgot, I wouldn't have been allowed to live in Hong Kong, but I do wonder, occasionally, what the house Mr. Mac Gowan offered me, would be like," and a shiver feathered her spine,

Aunt Daphne asking her first, if she was cold, for it was decidedly cooler up here and then to say,

"Cynicism doesn't suit you, Sarah. Put that disgraceful proposal out of your mind," severely.

They passed through a door that led on to another gallery, that ran around the four walls of a huge ballroom below. The room could easily accommodate twelve sets for the quadrille, ladies of the committee, seating guests, the flowers massed against one wall, foreign to Sarah and very beautiful. The scene below put Lady Weston's ballroom to shame.

"Ah," murmured Mr. Merton, just behind his wife, "I see Dick and his Agnes are here."

She nodded. "I believe the banns are to be called this Sunday," a contented sigh escaping her. "So nice to see their happiness," to continue smugly, "A very good turnout, I think," allowing her glance to roam about the vast room, "but then, who would ignore an invitation from the *tai-pan*? Our coffers will certainly, be filled again for the coming year, praise be!"

They began to descend the white, marble staircase, that widened considerably to the bottom, the bannisters and supports, of highly polished brass, Sarah whispering to Aunt Daphne, "And you expect me not to gaup at this this — ?" words failing her.

"Thought you might be impressed," she replied with satisfaction. "Don't you agree that this is the only venue for our ball?"

Nothing that Aunt Daphne had told her, had prepared her for this opulence, as guests thronged the floor and mingling with them, were soldiers and sailors in full dress uniform, standing out amongst the more soberly attired male guests, in black evening wear and pristine frilly shirts.

"I'm sure, Miss Danbury, you never expected anything like this," said a little lady next to her. "One runs out of superlatives in a mansion, such as this," dropping her voice, "but it is said that Simon Mac Gowan uses it to store his merchandise, three hundred and sixty four days of the year. Scandalous!"

At the foot of the stairs, the *tai-pan* and another committee member were welcoming the guests again, the Navy and Army band playing soft, background music. Their host had chosen to wear a light blue velvet coat, with edgings of silver lace, trousers to match, to stand out like a peacock amongst the peahens. This naughtily, from Sarah.

He had faced the prospect of a very dull evening, but as it was for a charitable organisation, he had been willing to do his part.

He turned to glance over the assembled company. Surely the list must be coming to its end and noticed a fair haired lady, whom he did not know, watching him over her fan, who was particularly fetching in a gold embroidered, red gown and long green gloves.

He raised a hand, which she acknowledged. At least he would have some entertainment to relieve all this forced affability and prised his glance from the lady's décolleté. Ah well, all in a good cause and only happened once a year.

He turned back and caught sight of Mr. and Mrs. Merton. He had not expected Sarah and his senses stirred, the red lady forgotten. She was a beautiful, graceful woman as she approached him with a friendly smile, her hair a rosy-gold nimbus, under the hundreds of candles in the great crystal chandeliers and experienced a stab of regret, that he had been such a crass fool. How could he have not recognised her virtue, wondering again if this lovely woman would accept a proposal of marriage from him. What a gracious mistress she's make in his home. Mistress, he had better be careful of that word, he thought ruefully, remembering that setdown she had given him; it was unusual for him to be so uncertain. What a wonderful mother she would make too, for his legitimate son, for he had to produce an heir to inherit his large fortune and eventually, to take over his numerous business ventures and acknowledged, that he wasn't getting any younger. He would take her sailing again, as she had really enjoyed that afternoon and this time he would not rush his fences. All this raced through his brain as he took her hand in his.

"Welcome, Miss Danbury," he said formally, with a bow. "Please keep me the first two waltzes," only a tautening of his facial muscles, betraying his previous thoughts. "I hope you enjoy the ball," scribbling his name against the dances. The evening that had been just another bore, now assumed a new dimension and his eyes gleamed.

The Mertons and Sarah passed on to be welcomed again by Mrs. Hill, who was his hostess for the evening, a kindly, motherly woman who smiled at Sarah, congratulating her on her dress, to remark dryly that there were some who had no right to be here.

At last the ball was opened by their host, the band striking up the first dance, Mr. Mac Gowan claiming Sarah's hand as he raised her from her chair, Aunt Daphne nodding and if it was not as friendly as it should have been, no one noticed. Earlier, her spouse had made good his escape to the card rooms.

The *tai-pan* smiled down at his partner, lightly clasping her slim waist, but firmly, as he swept her into the rhythm of the waltz, his first words, "Have you forgiven me yet, Miss Danbury?" and at her slight nod, "you are very beautiful tonight," he murmured.

However, Sarah would not play his little game. "Mr. Mac Gowan, please don't waste flowery commonplace on me. I love the waltz, so please let's forget the past," and with that Simon had to be content.

He was an excellent dancer and

they both gave themselves over to the magic of the lovely waltz and nothing more contentious was said. The dance ended and he took her back to Mrs. Merton.

Several seats further along, were the two Finch sisters, both teachers, discussing the dancing. "Miss Danbury and the *tai-pan* make such a lovely couple," said the younger of the two. "He's a Viking, with that head of fair hair and that beard, don't you agree, Jane?" with a wistful sigh.

"Nonsense, Esmerelda! Mr. Mac Gowan is a Scotsman and a very shrewd one at that," a little impatiently.

"But not clutch-fisted, sister. He would make an excellent husband for her," thinking back over the years of her lost love. He had been a shop assistant and her father had squashed that blossoming, "though, she's very cool towards him, don't you think?"

"Miss Danbury is behaving as she should and I hope she takes him down a peg or two. He's always far too cocky for my liking and I think he's overdressed," was her tart reply and characteristic sniff of disapproval.

"There are some beautiful gowns here tonight," Esmerelda persisted enviously, glancing down at her simple, though good blue chiffon, which suited her fair colouring, an orchid pinned on one shoulder. "Oh, look Jane, there is Dick and Agnes, she's rather pretty in a childish sort of way, isn't she? It will be so nice to attend a wedding again," she said more cheerfully, to add, "Jane, you do realise that we're living on other folk's experiences?" to which Jane could only nod in agreement.

Silence reigned for some time between the sisters, until Esmerelda sat up straighter, to say with pleased surprise, "What on earth is Major Prentice doing in Hong Kong?" a pretty pink creeping into her cheeks, lending a sparkle to her grey eyes. "How strange!"

"Probably on furlough," Jane replied, also surprised to see the Major, whom they had known in Calcutta.

Hector arriving late had brought him to the ball. The major had had to take sudden, early retirement, because of family affairs, Hector mystified as to why John had wanted to visit Hong Kong, but was very pleased to welcome him, never-the-less.

It transpired that the Major had a fondness for little Miss Esmerelda Finch and was looking forward to seeing her once more, before leaving the East for good.

"Your compass is way out, John," with a teasing smile and lifted eyebrow. "From Calcutta you've certainly back tracked."

He chuckled. "Yes, but I really like Esmerelda, but was loath to propose to her, because of her overpowering sister," he confessed, "but I love her funny endearing ways."

"Afraid that Miss Jane would want to live with you and rule the roost?"

He nodded ruefully. "Something like that," he admitted.

The band had started up again. "Go

and ask her to dance now and pop the question," giving him a friendly push. "I must find a partner," and made his way to where Sarah was sitting.

She saw him approaching, remembering again, how warmly she had welcomed him. 'My friend was lost and now is found', cringing inwardly and because of this, her greeting was a little cool.

"My compliments, Miss Danbury and may I say, you're looking very lovely?" drawing her to her feet, but instead of leading her onto the dance floor, took her a little aside. "I hope you don't mind, if we sit this one out, but I need your help for a friend," and proceeded to tell her Major Prentice's story.

"But what can I do?" Sarah just pleased to be in his company.

"Could you talk to Jane and see how the land lies? Hopefully, she does not wish to return to England."

Sarah was looking around her. "I see that your friend is already dancing with Miss Esmerelda, a dear little lady, as bright as a button and still youngish. I know her quite well, as she's Harry's teacher. I'll go and see what I can find out," she said obligingly.

During the course of the conversation, Sarah was able to establish that Jane had been far happier in Calcutta, but that the climate had not suited her sister and so they had applied for teaching posts here in Hong Kong.

After talking about this and that for a while longer, Sarah excused herself, Hector strolling across to her and asked if she would like to dance, but she shook her head.

"Let's rather meet Major Prentice and Miss Esmerelda as they come off the floor. I'd also like to suggest that you invite us all to the refreshment room, as I've the answer, I hope, to their problems, but do you think the Major has popped the question yet?" a little anxiously.

The *tai-pan* had been an interested onlooker during this little charade, that had been enacted under his very nose.

All that he knew was, that he was jealous of Mr. Carew and a bile rose up to taunt him, so much so that the stem of his wine glass snapped.

Sophia moved closer to him, raising an eyebrow, laying a land on his sleeve, "You're jealous, my friend. Perhaps now we'll share a fellow feeling. Youth to youth," she taunted, her glance following Mr. Carew and Miss Danbury. "Simon, I haven't seen you lately?"

"I've been out of town," his reply blunt.

Sophia was magnificent in a figure hugging *cheongsam*, in green satin richly embroidered, tight skirt slit to her knee, her black hair elaborately styled with silk flowers and slippers of black velvet, jewel-studded.

She had sensed his coldness, but did not take heed. "My dear, you're looking positively murderous!" she purred.

"My concerns are of little importance to you, Sophia," dampeningly, but she did not agree. "Oh, but they are, if you would let me into your life," she replied archly.

This was too much, he bowed and excused himself.

Simon was dancing with Sarah again. "Now please tell me, what is going on?" his manner a little stiff.

She chuckled. "Major Prentice came over especially, to see the youngest Miss Finch again, before leaving for Britain on early retirement. He's épris in that direction," with her wide, beaming smile.

"But Esmerelda is at least five and thirty," a surprised protest breaking from him.

"*Tai-Pan*, love comes to all ages," twinkling at him. "I'm so glad for them, but with men, of course, it's different. They have to sew wild oats before they settle down," her mischievous eyes daring him to contradict her.

"Sweet torment, you're a rogue!" his good humour restored and as the dance had ended, pressed a kiss on her wrist, which she snatched away quickly. It had been a far warmer kiss than was allowable, her glance cool. He bowed, "Miss Danbury, your servant," a muscle twitching beside his thin mouth. This little English rose was not one whit impressed by his position, or his magnificent mansion. There was no envy in her, his grimace twisting into derisive mockery at himself.

Dick brought Agnes over to where Aunt Daphne and Sarah were sitting, both of them smiling happily, Aunt Daphne inviting them to sit down and tell her all their news, at which point Sarah was claimed for the next dance, which was a lively polka.

She was happy too and pleased that the community had taken Agnes to their hearts and that Mrs. Gilbert had kindly suggested that Agnes stay with her family, until her marriage and who was also acting as her chaperon for this evening. How very hospitable people were.

Sophia once again accosted Simon, a tiny frisson of fear warning her to tread carefully, for she did not know Simon in this cold mood, but even so, she placed a hand on his shoulder. "My dance, I think, *Tai-Pan*?" she said sweetly, "and there is nothing you can do about it."

"Piracy?" murmuring in her ear.

She gurgled, but quick to notice that his eyes sought out Sarah. "That little ingénue will bore you in a month."

"Perhaps," was all he permitted himself to say refraining from remarking that an English woman should not wear a Chinese gown, no matter how beautiful they were and anyway, her figure was far too opulent for such a style, but enjoying, for a moment, the shock on Miss Jane's face, as they passed her and could well imagine that moralist's thoughts.

The ball ended well after midnight, in a traditional manner, Sarah gazing up at the soaring grandeur of the staircase again, as they left the ballroom below. An unforgettable evening.

On the way home, Mr. Merton

335

yawned sleepily. "Sarah, do you now realize what you have missed, by turning down Simon Mac Gowan's outrageous offer?"

"Sir, I would have been housed in some distant Eastern country, no doubt. Remember?" she retorted cynically.

"But in equal luxury, of course!" quizzing her lazily.

"Mr. Merton, could you ever live in that — that mausoleum?" she demanded.

He shook his head, yawning again, leaving Aunt Daphne to say with some asperity. "I wouldn't, there's no feeling of a home about it, at all. Poor man, he's forgotten what real home comforts are all about," to add with gratification. "This year's ball, has turned out to be the most lavish and well attended affair, as ever we've held."

★ ★ ★

Major John Prentice and Miss Esmerelda Finch were married in St. John's

336

Cathedral one week later, by a special dispensation given by the Bishop of Hong Kong, enabling the couple to catch the P & O boat to Britain that day, the English community gathering around to give them a splendid wedding reception and several weeks later, Dick was married to his Agnes and the community could settle down to more mundane events.

One late afternoon, Mr. Merton sent a message to his wife, to say that Hector had gone down with a fever and would she please make up a bed for him, as he felt he could not leave a member of his staff to the mercies of the hotel management.

"Oh dear," murmured Aunt Daphne and soon she and Sarah were bustling around getting a room ready, giving certain orders to Mei-mei. "I do hope the dear man isn't too ill. I'll send a message around to the doctor to call later and we'll take turns to nurse him."

Mr. Merton arrived and he and Mr.

Briggs put their patient to bed, who was shivering uncontrollably.

"A large cup of hot tea, laced with rum," ordered Mr. Merton, which Dr Lambert verified when he arrived, also prescribing quinine, for it was definitely malaria.

For several days Hector was very ill, the ladies taking it in turn to nurse him and then one evening when Sarah went down to take over from Aunt Daphne, a sharp, half-smothered exclamation escaped her. Hector looked ghastly.

"He's not improving at all, Aunt Daphne," she wailed. "It's as if he's lost his will to live."

Aunt Daphne shook her head. "You have never nursed a malaria patient, it takes time. Anyway, his next dose is in a half hour's time," glancing at the small clock on the bedside table, rising tiredly, to her feet. "Call me if you should not be able to manage," and with that slipped away to her bed.

Sarah sat down in the chair Aunt Daphne had just vacated, drawing it closer to the bed and began to talk softly, the lamp casting weird shadows around the room. "I can't begin to describe what your kiss began to mean to me and those loving words, when Edward died. You wouldn't believe me, for you don't recognize who I am. Why?" she murmured in despair. "My love!" laying her head on his arm, her tears soaking his night shirt.

Hector suddenly tried to sit up, but fell back exhausted, muttering, "I left her standing there, all by herself. How could I have done that?" he groaned. "Dreaming again, but it is better than nothing, flying from that which I cannot escape or forget; memories."

"I walked to the conservatory, Hector dear," she replied softly and immediately he quietened down, but became restless again.

"I'll never see her again, she's Edward's bride," groaning again. "I can't bear it," his deep voice shaking weakly, his grip on her arms surprisingly strong, as he reared up, but only to fall back again, exhausted, his grip lessening.

"You don't have to bear it, Hector dear, I'm here," gathering him to her, brushing hair from his brow, that was wet with perspiration, waves of happiness radiating through her, but warned herself again, that he might not recognise her, when he came to his senses.

"Is it really you?" his eyes bright with the fever, his deep voice shaking strangely, which pulled at her heart-strings. "You won't leave me?" he pleaded. "I'm dreaming again," he groaned, turning away.

Sarah turned his head to her. "Hector, it is really I, not a figment of your imagination," shaking him gently. "I'll be here when you wake up," she soothed, "Go to sleep, my love," as she wiped his face with a damp flannel and had the satisfaction of seeing him turn over and fall into a natural sleep, a smile creeping over his face, her smile equalling his, rosy with joy.

Sarah glanced quickly at the clock to see that it was time for his medicine, but decided that sleep was best for him.

Aunt Daphne came in hours later, to find both her guests sleeping peacefully.

"Hector will soon recover now," said Aunt Daphne, after she had woken Sarah. "Come, my dear, you need a cup of tea and some breakfast."

7

AUNT DAPHNE and Sarah continued to take it in turns to visit the sickroom several times during the night. On one of these visits, Sarah stood looking down at her patient, love in her eyes, there was no need to hide it, for Hector was sleeping peacefully, thankful that he was making such good progress and went back to report to Aunt Daphne, before she went up to bed, longing for the time when he would recognize her, so that she could tell him that she was willing to go wherever the government would send him. Was this just another of her fanciful dreams? Why, why, had he not recognised her, but still stubbornly adamant that she would not tell him who she was.

And Hector? As time passed he began to realize what a lovely person Miss Danbury was and began to wonder why he couldn't just accept what had happened at Edward's betrothal ball and fall in love with this charming young woman, but his mind would not accept this. He sighed and hoped that Edward and his bride were happy.

One night, very late, Sarah feeling particularly sad, her spirit at its lowest ebb, tiptoed downstairs into the drawing-room to open the grand piano and began to play softly. She was unaware how long she sat there, playing bits and pieces from the great composers, that soothed her, peace once again, descending upon her senses.

"Why do you stop," came a quiet voice from the sofa.

She spun around, startled, she hadn't even heard the door opening. Hector was stretched out comfortably, looking much better.

"Mr. Carew, do you think you should be up?" she asked anxiously, going to him.

He nodded, holding out his hand, taking hers in his warm clasp, to pull her down beside him, Sarah feeling that he was too close for comfort and that she had not remembered those wings of grey at his temples, either.

"My name is Hector, Miss Sarah and thank you for some excellent music. I'd also like to take the opportunity of thanking you for nursing me," and as she inclined her head, added, "I've recovered far quicker from this bout, than any other I have suffered," with deep gratitude.

"I'm very glad," she replied simply. "I thought you were asleep, otherwise I wouldn't have disturbed you, but it is good to see you up," rising to her feet. "Now, I think it is time you went back to bed."

Hector made a good recovery, blessing the Mertons for their hospitality. It would have been sheer hell, if he had had to stay in the hotel.

The following morning, Sarah was not at breakfast, Aunt Daphne going up to see the reason why, to find Sarah crumpled on the window seat, in deep despondency. She paused, the query on her tongue stilled as she searched Sarah's face. "What on earth has happened to distress you so?" gathering her guest into her arms, to hold her tawny head against her shoulder.

Sarah gulped, the whole story tumbling out; her betrothal to Edward, the ball, the stranger, who had kissed her so sweetly, who said that he would love her all his life, Edward's tragic death, to end with, "Mr. Carew is that stranger, Aunt Daphne," she hiccupped, drawing away a little. "I've lived with these memories for months. Why did he not recognise me?" she wailed.

"What a tale, child!" the words as gentle as her hand clasp, as if she herself was experiencing that hurtful rejection. A silence fell on the sunfilled bedroom, as Sarah tried to gather herself together, blowing her nose and drying her eyes.

Aunt Daphne was appalled and for a moment could only look at Sarah with deep pity and concern. "What you have had to bear! I sensed when I first met you, that you did not have an easy life, for why else would you, a gently reared girl, wish to find employment?"

"But what can I do?" she murmured, her lips quivering.

Aunt Daphne's reply was bracing. "What I can't understand is why you didn't tell Hector who you were, when you first met, you stubborn child!" her glance keen.

Sarah sat up with a gasp, her voice totally suspended, recovering it again to say with a watery sniff, "I could never be so forward!" shaking her head firmly.

"Why ever not?" challenged Aunt Daphne. "You love him, don't you?" she countered forthrightly.

She nodded, "But sometimes I've wondered if the whole incident wasn't a huge joke played on Edward, or perhaps Hector had regretted his actions?"

The elder of the two snorted. "What utter nonsense!"

"If Mr. Carew had really meant what he said, why didn't he come to find me after Edward's death? He must have known about it. Oh!" surprised, "he doesn't know, for he told me that he hadn't had any mail directed to him from the Calcutta office, since arriving here in Hong Kong, but that doesn't change anything," she said obstinately. "Mr. Carew did not recognize me at your party; his eyes are too kindly to be devious. He must have caught the boat to Hong Kong, soon after the ball."

A silence fell, Aunt Daphne the one to eventually break it. "Now I wonder why Hector didn't recognize you? There must be something significantly different about you now." Another pause. "If we can dress you exactly as you were that night, your hair — "

"My hair!" Sarah sat up straighter. "Louise did it in a very fancy style, oh, I remember now. Do you think, Aunt Daphne, this is the answer?" her face alight with warmth again.

Aunt Daphne nodded. "You always

dress your hair very simply, now Hector is going to meet you as he saw you at that ball and we'll give you the biggest wedding Hong Kong has ever seen! I couldn't be more pleased if you were my own daughter. Bless you!" her smile decidedly mischievous.

Sarah hugged her, too overcome for words, but managed, at last, to say, a little apprehensively, "You won't speak of this to anyone else, please," she insisted. "It could all go so sadly wrong."

Aunt Daphne agreed, her thoughts running ahead. "The Governor's Ball is to be held soon, I'll ask Hector to be your escort and we'll do your hair in that same style and now for the dress, please describe it so we can have one made up quickly, in the same style and colour."

With a touch of wizardry, Sarah rushed to the wardrobe to bring out her betrothal gown. "Priscilla, my niece, bless her, insisted that I pack this, just in case and how right she was!"

joy taking the place of tears.

"What a beautiful dress," breathed Aunt Daphne. It was in the palest peach mousseline, with a wide scalloped neckline and tiny puffed sleeves. The outer dress was knee length, to show off the flounces of the satin petticoat in a darker shade. "How very providential," was all she found to say, but her mind was rushing ahead. "Before we leave for the ball, Hector will be shown into the drawing-room and then," with an impish smile, as her plan unfolded, "make your entrance. *Voilà!*" throwing up her hands, "and all will be made known," ending on a triumphant note.

"Aunt Daphne, you're a dear genius!" hugging her.

"My dear, what a romance," she sighed soulfully. "No wonder that poor boy has been so quiet, he's had no hope. Also Sarah, don't forget that he thinks you are married to Edward and certainly did not expect to find you here."

"But what if he wasn't serious?" doubts coming to the fore again to trouble her.

"Put such thoughts out of your mind, my girl. Don't you realize that he is being true to his love, for the girl he met at your ball? Now, don't you think that you should have breakfast?"

The days that followed were not easy ones for Sarah, even though her hopes were high. She attended dances, alfresco parties and even attended the races, this with Hector. It was here that they met Mr. Mac Gowan, who had been out of town again.

He stopped and the usual greetings voiced, before Hector congratulated and thanked him for a magnificent ball. "I'll always remember it because John Prentice was able to pop the question and retire with the lady of his dreams."

The *tai-pan* nodded briefly, "With your connivance, no doubt, Carew?" casting a smouldering glance at Sarah's happy face, to say coldly, "I suppose,

Miss Sarah, that you are friendly with Carew because of his expectations of a title?" with a sneer.

Sarah could only stare at him. It was plain to see that he did not like Mr. Carew, but need he be quite so bad mannered, not understanding the bitterness that filled him, because, even with his vast wealth, he could not buy himself into the aristocracy, for which his soul craved.

Hector chuckled. "Mr. Mac Gowan, you've got the wrong sow by the ear. I've no expectations. Old lambchops is only about three years my senior. No luck there! I'm not in the direct line, anyway."

Sarah was appalled and could only stand mum-chance. Surely the *tai-pan* wasn't jealous?

The invitations for the Governor's Ball were received and the small community could talk of nothing else, but the long awaited day did arrive, Sarah unable to settle to anything, until Aunt Daphne exasperated, shooed her out of the house, suggesting she take Hong for a walk and rid herself of her fidgets. By the time the dog had pulled her into the shopping area, they were both out of breath. Several times, the animal had snarled, showing a splendid set of teeth, whenever someone advanced too close to her.

Sarah had become quite as well known as Miss Merrow and Sparks, her pug. Several people had asked her kindly what she would do with Hong when she returned home. Sarah had wondered about that too, but comforted herself with the assurance that Mr. Briggs would oblige, her thoughts so far away, that when Hector touched her arm, she turned around in fright.

"It's only me," he soothed, to add abruptly, "Where's your maid," looking around for Mei-mei, his disapproval plain to see.

"She's busy pressing all our clothes for tonight's ball," but that did not appease him.

"You would not go out unattended in London."

"Perhaps not, but I don't see why you should worry about me," her usual smile absent, her apprehension on the outcome of this evening's meeting, making her a trifle abrupt.

"People in small cities like this, are sticklers as far as conventions are concerned, far more so than they would be at home."

Sarah relented, she could not help herself, a twinkle peeping through. "I have a protector," glancing down at the dog. "Please be easy."

"I know, Hong has certainly turned out to be a fine mongrel," giving the animal a friendly pat. "I'm looking forward to being your escort this evening, Miss Sarah," he added with a smile, "but now I really must excuse myself. As usual, I'm out on government business," lifting his hat. He gave Hong another pat, with an admonition to look after his mistress and then strode away.

Hector had been invited to an early dinner, arriving looking very distinguished in a black suit, his cravat and silk shirt pristine, his gold cuff-links plain, Mr. Merton begging pardon for the early hour, as the ladies had decided to dress after the meal.

How wonderful it would be if Hector would bend down and kiss her, thought Sarah, but her words of greeting gave no hint of her inner excitement. How could Aunt Daphne be so calm, even Mr. Merton, the most placid of men, felt the tension. Naturally, he had been told of Sarah's romance, but his good manners were not affected as he chatted pleasantly to their guest during the meal, until the ladies excused themselves.

Aunt Daphne and Mei-mei helped Sarah to dress, again admiring her beautiful gown. "You're a lovely person, my dear and my blessing go with you, but now I must go and dress myself," bending over to kiss her. "Mei-mei will do your hair," and with that she disappeared, her eyes moist, but for all that, Sarah could not be easy.

What if Hector had not remembered her, the time lapse being too long and he had forgotten the young girl he had kissed so sweetly, forgotten the words he had uttered? She would soon find out if it had all been a hoax.

Sarah gave the little *amah* instructions on how to style her hair in a topknot, encircling it with a garland of silk amber roses, allowing curly strands to fall on either side of her face, her fringe cut low from under which peeped her apprehensive eyes.

"Plenty men talky talky you," grinned Mei-mei, with a satisfied nod and when Sarah brought out her mother's pearl necklace, Mei-mei could only stare in admiration, finally breaking into her own language, to say that she must now go and help the madam.

Great trepidation and high hopes accompanied Sarah as she entered the drawing-room. At her appearance, Mr. Merton took his wife's arm, excusing themselves and when the door was shut said, "Give that young couple a chance to sort out their own lives, my dear, it doesn't do to meddle."

"Meddle, me? I wanted to see Hector's reaction when he first knows who she is," she replied indignantly.

"Yes, dear, you want to see everyone happy," he soothed kindly.

Sarah had given Hector a shy smile, showing her vulnerability, knowing that it would break her heart, if he did not recognise her.

It was as if time had stopped and they were alone in the whole world and then he was on his feet, knocking over the wineglass. "Is it you, my love?" he breathed, astonishment and hope lighting up his eyes, that roamed her face to assure himself that she was the same girl to whom he had made that declaration of love, so many months ago. Two hasty strides brought him to her. "My dearest dear, this isn't another dream, is it?" with a look of wonderment as he came closer, to gently touch her face, with gentle fingers.

Whatever doubts had assailed Sarah, vanished. "It was at a certain betrothal ball," she said quietly, "when a certain young man approached a certain engaged lady," that was as far as she was allowed to go.

He scooped her into his arms, to hold her in a crushing embrace. "My love, my love, it is you," as if he would never let her go, his face close to hers. "Never in my wildest dreams did I think I would ever find you again." He suddenly drew back in astonishment. "Miss Danbury?" just realizing who she was. "Edward, what of Edward?" his voice harsh, "I've got to be dreaming again. What happened?" his arms falling.

"Mr. Carew, please sit down. I've much to tell you," she said gently, leading him back to the sofa.

"Hector," he said automatically, his brows knitted, but still retaining her hand. "Edward is dead, isn't he?"

357

Sarah nodded mutely, Hector drawing her gently to him again, laying his head against hers. "Did you love him?"

"No, no!" a shudder running through her slim body, that he was quick to feel. "It was an arranged affair and not one to my liking especially, dear Hector, after that very satisfying kiss of yours," she teased.

"Oh lor' my brother is next in line! His paws are going to be nicely buttered. Who would have thought it!"

"Do you mean to say that you are related to the Weston family?" startled. "Yes, I suppose that is why you were at the ball."

He nodded soberly. "Damn the Calcutta office for not redirecting my mail. Edward was killed in a riding accident, wasn't he?"

Sarah looked at him in surprise. "How did you know?"

"I didn't, but he was always a bruising rider. Poor Aunt, she must be feeling his death keenly and on top of that has not heard from me."

"My grieving was for Lady Weston. What a dear she is and she's going to be charmed with our news, dear Hector," to pause horrified. "Oh, goodness, I've presumed too much," delightful colour sweeping her face, Hector acting promptly.

"Will you marry me, Miss Sarah Danbury? I want to know how far that blush goes down," with an appreciative glance at her low cut gown, chuckling. "As soon as the banns are called, we'll take the next boat," kissing her with swift gentleness, finding a quivering answering warmth that he hoped for. "And I had thought I had lost you, my love. Why didn't I recognise you?" he groaned.

"You only saw me for a few minutes and my hair was done differently. This is how I was dressed and my hair done in the same style and you recognised me. I was banking on that," she murmured lovingly.

Aunt Daphne knocked and peeped

around the door, heaving a huge sigh at the sight of their happy faces. "Praise be, I see you've found each other. Congratulations," giving them both a hug, Hector saying,

"Mrs. Merton, we must go back home and will be married as soon as possible," telling her why.

Aunt Daphne nodded. "My dears, I'd like to suggest that you announce your engagement tonight. William will speak to His Excellency and ask for compassionate leave for you. Now come, my dears, it is time for us to leave. You can tell us all about it in the carriage. Hector, please join my husband in his study, to discuss your plans and Sarah dear, you'd better go and tidy that head of yours."

THE END

WITH SOMEBODY
Theresa Charles

Rosamond sets off for Cornwall with Hugo to meet his family, blissfully unaware of the shocks in store for her.

A SUMMER FOR STRANGERS
Claire Hamilton

Because she had lost her job, her flat and she had no money, Tabitha agreed to pose as Adam's future wife although she believed the scheme to be deceitful and cruel.

VILLA OF SINGING WATER
Angela Petron

The disquieting incidents that occurred at the Vatican and the Colosseum did not trouble Jan at first, but then they became increasingly unpleasant and alarming.